Great Alaskan Shorts

Short Stories and Poetry from the Last Frontier

James Guenther

DEDICATION

There are many people who I wish to thank for their help with this book. I thank my extended family, especially my four wonderful sisters, who have always encouraged my writing and painting. To my wife, Barbara, who let me have the time to work on this book, and who seldom pulled me from my studio and asked me to stop and rejoin the world; and when she did, it was always a good thing. To my kids, Danielle, Lucas, Briana and Jacob, who, having given me a great number of grey hairs, have also kept me young at heart, taught me to see the world in a new light, and have enveloped me in their love. I thank the many friends who have encouraged me along the way; especially to our good friends, Don and Nancy Mitchel, who know how to give support just by flexing certain muscles in their faces, causing smiles to replace doubts. I thank the Ketchikan Area Arts and Humanities Council who had enough confidence in me to grant me an exhibition of my paintings and sculpture that accompanied some of my writing, which in turn, gave me the impetus to finish and compile many of the poems and stories in this book. And finally I wish to thank my parents who are no longer with me, but who gave me so much love and encouragement, that no dedication on my part could ever fully express my profound appreciation for the gifts and lessons they so generously gave.

An Introduction by the Author

When I first decided to compile these stories and poems I had no idea as to the intensity of commitment it would require. I just had a dream; to have a public art show of my paintings and to relate some of them to a few poems that I had been working on. As in all endeavors, one thing leads to another, and everything changes everything else, until, in the end, nothing is quite what it was in the beginning.

During the summer of 2012 I took members of my family on a pilgrimage across Spain. It was somewhere along the Camino Santiago that the idea for this book began to take shape. On that walk I learned many lessons. Among them I learned how to be patient. Walking an average of fifteen miles a day for thirty-three days gave me time to put my priorities in line. I learned to watch for signs and grew to believe that there are signs leading us to our destiny, if only we are careful to look for them. I learned that, like the thousands of pilgrims on the Camino, everyone in life walks for their own purpose and at their own pace. I came to understand that we are all born with a talent that we are intended to share, and that it often takes an act of courage to share our talents.

This project took on a life of its own, and now that I'm giving birth to it, it kind of hurts. There is a lot of myself in these pages. As with any art, whether it is sung or danced, played or painted, acted, or sculpted, or written, it is very personal. It is a tribute to our humanity that we are willing to glorify it, to expose it, to define it, to make light of it. If our art makes us think about our lives and our place the universe, then it is worthy of us to share it. It takes courage to throw it out there. I hope that other artists see this work and say, "I have a talent. I have courage. I will share my talents, too." And then I hope they do.

The poetry and stories in this book were the inspiration for my exhibition "Painted Poems". Each of the stories are little, one acre fields of fiction, planted with tiny seeds of truth, grown in the fertile manure of my mind. A few of the tales are very loosely based on actual events and so the names, circumstances, and characters have been changed to protect the innocent.

On a side note, I can't blame anyone else for this book. I did the layout, the editing, the design, everything. The voices in it are mine. I wanted this book to be one hundred percent my work, and so it is. I've made up a few words just because I like the way they sound. I know that I could edit, and edit, and edit until hell freezes over, and that even then, there will still be typos and awkward sentences.

But sometimes things just need to get born and they can't wait for the perfect time. So here it is and I hope you enjoy it.

Jim Guenther
August 27, 2013

Table of Contents

Transcendencia

At the zenith of creativity
There emerges a vibrant clarity.
Generated from a place
Beyond the Self.

The background world disintegrates
Into a mass of superficial grey.
While an invisible hand,
A specter's wand
Illuminates truth.

Casting about shadows,
Gathering light from darkness,
And coloring thought.

How One-Eyed Willy Lost His Luck

Trapper Hogsdale burst into the one-room schoolhouse like a second grade tornado. Papers were sucked off their desks and fluttered in his wake.

"Schoolteachew!" he hollered too loudly. "Teachew!" he screamed at me with his r-dropping, speech impeded drawl. "Willy just backed the camp twuck off the float plane wamp and he's in the bay!"

"Again?" I asked as I jumped up from my desk. I ran over to my window and looked out onto the playground.

"Yeppews," Trapper replied seriously. "The twuck is in the dwink."

All of the children had run to the far end of the playground and were pointing excitedly toward the dock.

Missus Prissy, my classroom aide, was lumbering to catch up. I'd never before seen Missus

Prissy run and found it to be a bouncing spectacle of motion. I was struck with the déjà vu recollection of a dancing hippopotamus floating gracefully to Amilcare Ponchielli's *Dance of the Hours*; her enormous, pulsating being overflowing the boundaries of straps and belts in total disregard for the laws of motion prescribed by Sir Isaac Newton.

"Let's go and see," I said to Trapper but he had already spun around and was flying back out the door. Like me, Trapper didn't want to be the only one in the home-guard of the Crusty Bay Logging Camp not to witness this extraordinary event.

When we arrived at the edge of the rock pad of the camp we witnessed the commotion. Barry, the floatplane pilot, was unloading freight from his DeHavilland Beaver as if nothing out of the ordinary had happened. I guessed that he had seen a great many calamities in his decades of supplying freight and mail to the numerous logging camps scattered throughout southern southeast Alaska. But off to the side of the ramp, in the cold water, was One-Eye Willy. He was splashing, and wavin' his arms around, and cussin' loud enough so that Missus Prissy cupped her hands over little Carrot McDoogal's pink ears. The chrome headlights of the red camp truck could be seen slowly sinking down into Crusty Bay.

"Leave me be, Mithuth Prithy", squirmed Carrot, "I've heard worth cuthin' from my Grandma." And she spun back around to catch the action, whipping Missus with her bright orange braids of hair.

Too-Tall Tom, the Camp Boss, was standin' at the top of the dock lookin' as mean as a bear with his hands on his hips and shakin' his head.

"That dad gum truck!" Willy gasped between bobs. His iconic white sailors cap was down over his eyes. It was hard to hear just what he was cussin' about on account of his mouth was under water for every other word.

Pretty soon he must have discovered that he'd made it up to the shallows because he stood up and took off his hat and started splashin' water every which way, but mainly in the direction from which the truck had so recently slipped beneath the surface.

"You're fired," yelled Too-Tall. He then turned on his heels and headed back up to the bunkhouse.

"Aaaagain," all the children chanted in unison.

"You kids git!" shouted Willy. "Git on back to the schoolhouse. There's nothing to see here. You jes' go on an' git!"

But we just had to stay and watch. Never mind the fact that nothing I could teach that afternoon would stick to their youthful brains longer than the visions of One-Eye Willy trying to rescue the camp truck. Besides, all of their mothers, and the tree thinners, and the hook tenders who had just come back on the early crummy were gathering about on the landing as if it were a Fourth of July picnic. Jake Strong was on his radio calling the Siderod, Curly, to hurry his crew back to camp for we all knew we were in for a treat.

What happened next went something like this...

Willy sloshed himself up to the sort yard and got the keys to an enormous log loader. He started it up and with the diesel stacks spewing black smoke, and the giant claw arms swinging to and fro, he came haulin' down the hill so fast and wild that some folks had to jump into the ditch.

We all were thinking that Willy was going to try and take the big Caterpillar log-loader down the ramp and some men were taking bets as to how long a loader would teeter on the float plane dock before it would flip over. Barry looked nervous and started to untie his Beaver.

Just then Too-Tall Tom came running back down the hill waving his arms. Willy stopped the machine and the two of them spoke a few colorful words. Tom waved his arms a lot, and Missus Prissy cupped Carrot's ears again. Then Tom stormed off and Willy crawled down out of the loader and grabbed a long, yellow, nylon-web tow strap and started walking back into the water with it wrapped around his waist. Pretty soon he was up to his shoulders, then his neck, and then all we could see was his little, white sailors cap floating all alone in the drink.

From our high vantage we had the perfect seats. In the clean Alaska salt water we could make out the red truck and Willy swimming like a pond frog toward it. He must have run out of breath though, because he came shooting to the surface like a breaching humpback. He swum over and fetched up his little white hat and turned to the crowd who were all loitering about and he smiled and said, "I jus' come up fer my hat." And with a heroic wave, he kicked his feet up over his head and dove back down to the truck. We could see him putting that yellow strap around the front axle before he surfaced again.

Willy surfaced triumphantly. Then Barry the pilot yelled to him, "Willy, that truck is still in reverse. You ought to take it out of gear before you try pullin' it back up here with the loader."

Willy raised his hand in a gesture of understanding then pulled his hat down hard over his ears and went upside down again and was kickin' for the truck.

We could vaguely see him swim in through the drivers' window, his feet dangling upward. He must have used one hand to push in the clutch, and the other to take the truck out of gear. Again he rose triumphantly to the surface, to his adoring fans, and to the bellowing crowd.

We were waving at him like crazy people and he was smiling and proud. He would have taken a big bow if he'd been up on the dry land, but as it was he just waved that crazy hat and smiled as big as all get out. Just then he realized what we were all yelling.

"Willy! There goes the camp truck!"

When Willy had taken the truck out of gear it had slowly started rolling backward under water and we all knew that Crusty Bay dropped off to something around four hundred feet deep.

Suddenly Willy wasn't smiling any more. He started tugging in earnest at the yellow strapping, which he had threaded through its own end and around his waist. He was kicking like mad and then he started hollering. He was getting farther and farther from shore and then, suddenly, he was just plain gone, like nothing had ever even been there.

The crowd on the dock went silent. The kids were even quiet. Everyone just looked out toward Crusty Bay. Barry, the pilot took off his ball cap and placed it over his heart. Little Carrot Mc Doogal buried her face in Missus Prissy's gigantic stomach and sobbed.

"Poor ol' One-Eye," someone in the crowd whispered.

And then he reappeared. Willy shot up to the surface exactly like that trained orca does at the Sea World Show down in San Diego. It was truly spectacular. Water droplets formed a beautiful, arching rainbow.

The crowd went wild! Women cried for joy and men slapped one another on their backs, and the children all started yelling, "It's Willy! He's alive! He's alive!"

Willy swam to shore and was helped out of the water by some of the bunkies. Who, I noticed, had just exchanged some money over the outcome of the event. He was a hero and before I called the children back inside to clean up and dismiss, we saw the men hoist Willy on their shoulders and carry him up the hill to the Grub Shack. Everyone was shouting 'Hurrahs' and generally having a grand ol' time.

*   *   *

Just to be clear about one thing, One-Eye Willy didn't have just one eye. He had two, just like you and me. But probably NOT just like you, or me, Willy's eyes were of two different colors; one was brown, and the other was blue. Now this shouldn't technically make a difference in how an eye functions, but Willy swore that he saw things differently through those two eyes. And everyone in Crusty Bay knew it had somehow altered his depth perception because he was the very worst driver in the whole world.

One afternoon, while I was checking for mail down at the camp office, Willy explained it to me this way:

"This 'n'," he'd said while pointing up to his brown eye, "sees in the light. And this 'n', sees in the dark," he said ominously while pointing to his pale blue eye. "But it'll see thin's thet nobody else'll ever see. Thin's thet nobody else would WANT to see."

"Like what?" piped one of the new bunkies in the hiring line. "You're big ugly butt?"

"Har, har, har, you think yer funny now, fella, but ya won't be laughin' fer long."

And then I witnessed skinny, ol' One-Eye step right up, face to face with that big, mean-looking new man. And Willy shook his head hard. And he looked up into that newcomers eyes and he said, "No. You won't be laughin' at all."

"You are plumb crazy," the stranger said. But I could tell that One-Eye had given the man the heebie-jeebies. Nobody is as superstitious as a logger. Especially a young choker setter who has to crawl around and under felled trees as big as freight trains and hook 'em up to a yarder cable and duck underneath them as they go flying overhead in a slip noose, or crashing down to the landing swinging their mighty trunks mere inches overhead. No sir, nobody's more superstitious than a choker setter.

The line crept forward as a gal finished using the only phone in camp to order her groceries from the Petersburg store. I waited patiently as J.T., the office manager, took the new hires' social security numbers and filled out their paperwork. One-Eye was behind me actin' nervous as a cat.

"The company has an insurance program," J.T. was explaining, "in case you get killed on the job. Sign right here for the hundred thousand dollar accidental death policy.

And right here," he continued, "write the name and a contact for your beneficiary."

The new man paused to think, "I sure as hell don't want my ex-wife to get any of it."

He looked around the office then turned to the next guy in line, Mad Max Crow. Max was a regular in the new hire line because he'd get fired about every two weeks for breaking the Dry Camp Rule. "Hey what's yer name, Pard?" the stranger asked Max, And then he said, "Fill this form in, 'cause you're my new beneficiary."

When it was finally my turn in line J.T. handed me my mail and I left quickly. It was the very next day when I heard that the new man, the one who had chided Willy and then had picked a perfect stranger to be his beneficiary, had been killed suddenly when a big, cedar tree with a rotten core kicked out of the sling and fell on him. Not long afterwards, Mad Max, the beneficiary, took his best chum, Dog-Ear Dan, and his hundred thousand dollar insurance payment, and headed out for Vegas and the good life. (They were back in line to get work at Crusty Bay within two months and neither one had two nickels to rub together. They had wrecked a brand new Corvette and had landed in a Nevada jail cell, but overall they said that they'd had just a wonderful time.)

We all were beginning to think that maybe ol' One-Eye did see things differently than most folks.

*   *   *

One day not long after he'd sunk the red truck, I found One-Eye at the camp office. He looked terrible! J.T. had just sat him down by the map table and was administering oxygen. Willy was a mess, covered with mud from head to toe.

"Holy Crap! What the heck happened to you?" J.T. asked.

Willy sucked on the big green oxygen bottle. I'd never seen a man in such a state. Both of his eyes, the brown and the dull blue one, where bulging in their sockets. His wrinkly old neck was bright red, but his face was ghastly pale. I knew then and there that Willy was going to die

"Look J.T.! Willy's hair has all turned gray!" I shouted, "He's turned into an old man... WOW, just look at how old and gray he looks J.T., and his neck's getting' even redder! I don't think he's going to make it, J.T. I'm sure he's going to die right here."

Willy tried to say something but he couldn't seem to catch his breath. Then he started speaking laboriously   between   puffs   of   oxygen.

"I...have...had...gray...hair...for...many...years...you...stupid...jack..."

"Whoa, I know what's different! Willy, where is your little white sailors cap?"

"That's it!" affirmed J.T, "This is the first time I've ever seen Willy without that cap. Gee wiz, One-eye, Where's your cap?"

"Bars... got...it." Willy puffed.

"What do you mean the bars got it? What the crap happened to you Willy?" J.T. asked.

Willy was taking deeper breaths now and started in on the terrible tale.

"Too-Tall Tom asked me to take the scraps from the Grub Shack out to the garbage pit," Willy began, "so's to keep the bars out o' camp. Well, when I got out thar, thar was nineteen bars in the pit. I was havin' a good ol' time parked up on the top of the cut with all them bar down below me in the pit. I was chuckin' spaghetti at 'em, and tossin' 'em stale bread and steak bones. I was throwin' flapjacks like Frisbees and them bars was catchin' 'em in their mouths like little hippy dogs. I was hollerin' 'Fetch this 'er, ya dumb bar.' And they was a getting' more an' more excited, like the white sharks on the TV, you know, all worked up. Pertty soon, two ol' boars started fightin' over a half a can o' beans. Then all them bars started growlin' an' takin' swipes at one another."

" Well, that truck o' Tom's, what with the tailgate down, an' on a slight decline, an' what with them broke down cardboard boxes underneath everthin' in the bed. I jus' started slidin' thets all. My feet shot out from unner me, an' I landed on my back and slid down thet cardboard and went shootin' offa the tailgate right through the air! An' I landed right der in thet pit full o' bars."

"And then, fer just a second, everthin' got ver', ver' quiet. All them bar jes' stopped what they wuz doin' an' looked at me. They looked at me like I was a Bone-in-Ham!"

"An' then thet big boar come. They had me outnumbered nineteen to one, an playin' dead didn't seem like no fun neither, seein's how everthin' they'd been eatin' was already dead. So I decided to make a run fer it. Thet big un come an' took my hat, an' if I hadn't ducked he'd o' took my head with it."

"So he and his buddy was fightin' o're my good luck hat. An' I wanted it back real bad, but then an thar, I made up my mind to let them bar have my hat. I knowed that my good luck hat was using all its' power so's I could escape and I watched in horror as THET BAR ET MA LUCKY HAT!"

"It was time to skedaddle! I don' recollect how I clawed my way up outta that pit. Well, you've seen it J.T. It's gotta be fo' o'five yads deep an' straight up an' down. Alls I can say is I flew outta that bar pit. Jesus saved me from them bar. I was saved by the mighty hand o' God Hisself, else I coulda never got out."

"You've seen that pit J.T. I've been saved! An' look at them holes in my boot!"

And sure enough there were three big tooth marks in the toe of his boot. I helped him take his boot off and besides having dented the steel toes a little bit, his foot was fine!

"Are you going to be alright, Willy? Is there anything we can get you?" JT and I were both concerned. He'd had a brush with death and he had come out on top.

"Well, yessiree fellas. You can git me on the next floatplane outta here. I'm gonna answer the call, Boys. I've got me some livin' to do!"

*   *   *

I met old One-Eye Willy several years later down in Ketchikan Town. He'd traveled to the orient and married a pretty Filipino gal. At seventy-three years of age he still enjoyed playing with his twelve beautiful children and besides all that, he ran the shelter for unemployed loggers, (Which was housing just about everyone I'd ever met in the timber industry.)

We went out that evening and had a few beers at the Arctic Bar. And just to hear that story one more time I asked him....

"Hey Willy, whatever happened to that goofy sailor hat that you always used to wear?"

As he related his story that last time I began to understand that One-Eye Willy's luck hadn't really been eaten by a bear that fateful day... just his hat.

Good Men and True

They're good men and true
The men who hew
The timber that floats to the mill.
Though their language is rough
They're an honest breed,
(When they haven't been hittin' the still.)

One weekend in March
When the wind blew cold,
I decided to take a break
And fly on in to Sitka-Town
To taste good beer and steak.

I ran down the ramp to the floatplane dock
And was lounging in the sun,
Dreamin' of getting' off o' this rock
And havin' me some fun.

Now life in a loggin' camp some say,
"Is hard." And that be true.
But workin' a camp like Rowan Bay
Is like sufferin' from the flu.

My thoughts were ended by a floatplane's roar
And I looked up to see BellAir.
"Take me to the P-Bar, Ken,
For I've some cash to spare."

The beaver danced on a foamy crest
Then leapt for the sapphire sky,
With none on board but the Holy Ghost,
The aviator, and I.

In the morning sun the majestic peaks
Of Baranov's eastern coast
Thrust frosty pinnacles skyward
As if reaching for The Host.

As we glided o're those lofty peaks
My heart was awe inspired,
And I made up my mind that I'd log no more
For I'd grown too fat and too tired.

And there, by God, I felt free at last
Beyond the siderod's stare,
And somewhere down below me
Was a gal with auburn hair.

We flew o're Silver Bay and then
I shouted, "There she be!"
And like a jewel on a rocky coast
Shone Sitka-by-the-Sea.

Now after days of heavy drinkin'
A man starts seein' clear,
Especially when the banks run dry
And you lose your taste for beer.

When gals with auburn hair turn sour
And you lose your sense o' humor,
And you find yourself reminiscin' camp
With all the home-guard rumors.

Then it's time to grab your ol' caulk boots
An' head for the dreary plane.
But if you find yourself back in Rowan Bay
You'll know that you must be insane.

We're good men and true,
The men who hew
The timber that floats to the mill.
Though our language is rough
We're an honest breed,
(When we haven't been hittin' the still.)

The Secret of Foggy Flats

It was early in November when mean, little Shorty McKracken unexpectedly approached Fuzzy and me in the Calamity Tavern. "Hey Schoolteacher, you boys want to go goose huntin' up Foggy Flats? I'm anchoring the *Lizzy-May* up there this week. You fellas can join me, or if you need to go to work, Schoolteacher, you can take your own danged boat," Shorty barked.

Thankfully, I did have to work Monday so Fuzzy and I agreed take my boat *The Miss Stake*. We liked Shorty, but in a cautious, self-preservative kind of way because Shorty was the most cantankerous man in the entire panhandle of Alaska. He didn't get his nickname just for being sixty inches tall but also because he had the shortest fuse of anyone I've ever met. He was one fella that you never wanted to get riled and there were bullet holes in the Calamity Tavern to prove it. If Shorty ever felt slighted, he would not forgive *or* forget. He carried a grudge with most folks in town, so people would walk on eggshells whenever he was about, and I, being new to Calamity Springs, was his new 'Pard'.

The next morning, Shorty's boat was just pulling away from the dock when Fuzzy and I arrived. "I'll see ya up there." Shorty scowled as the *Lizzy May* chugged beyond the breakwater. We could tell he was miffed that we were late. Any time after first light was too late as far as Shorty was concerned.

For the next three hours Fuzzy and I did what most fellas would do on a cruise up to Foggy Flats. We told each other lies. Somehow the topic got onto bear encounters. Everyone in Calamity Inlet has a few good bear stories to tell and Fuzzy and I were no exception.

My stories were all one hundred percent true facts that usually ended with a close call. Fuzzy's, on the other hand, were ominous in there horrible gore and bloody details. They were of the genre in which there were no heroes or survivors. Everyone in them was ripped apart and eaten. Fuzzy told each gruesome tale with a relish of description and action, or he would solemnly report that no traces of the bodies were ever recovered.

By the time we got to Foggy Flats we had spooked ourselves silly with the bear tales and I could tell that Fuzzy had become apprehensive about the hunt. Courage is a fleeting trait and had deserted us completely by the end of Fuzzy's diatribes. We were going into some mighty rugged country at the mouth of a salmon stream. And because it had been a mild fall, we both knew that some big Chichagof Island brownies were likely to be about.

After rafting up to the *Lizzy May*, we nervously set off for shore in the dinghy to search for Shorty. Fuzzy had strapped on his big 45 caliber pistol and kept one hand tight on the pearl grips as his beady eyes darted anxiously around the shoreline. He was a nervous fellow in any environment but today his grubby hands were shaking with tension. "I've heard of bears swimmin' out an' taken folks right out of their dinghies," Fuzzy warned.

Foggy Flats is the mouth of a river delta flowing into marshy tidelands. The beach grasses grow as tall as a man and are riddled with game trails. As we made our way through the wild and muddy terrain, Fuzzy stopped at every pile of scat and claw print to point out their incredible size then babbled unceasingly on the likelihood of meeting up with the monsters who'd made them.

After a while we began to worry about Shorty. We'd seen but few man tracks in the mud and still hadn't located him. "He's been taken by a bear for certain," was Fuzzy's conclusion as he climbed up on one of the many driftwood logs that had been deposited in the flats. From atop the log, Fuzzy peered out over the tall grass to survey the surrounding flats.

"There he is," whispered Fuzzy.

"A bear?" I whispered back..

"No, not yet. But they are out there somewhere, patient as vultures, waiting for us to make a mistake and then they'll come circling in to make the kill. In this high grass we won't see them till it's too late." Fuzzy whispered. "I'll save two bullets in the pistol to put us out of our misery while we're bein' eaten alive."

We both got very quiet and thoughtful then. I guess we were thinking about being eaten alive and having no choice but to do ourselves in or suffer in a terrible way.

"There's Shorty," he said with relief. "Come on."

Shorty was only a few yards away when we broke into a clearing where the recent flooding had laid the marsh grass flat. We found him crouching behind a driftwood snag looking out over the twenty or so goose decoys he had set up along the river.

I've got this place covered," he said. "You boys go on upstream a ways. There's an old beaver dam up there where I saw some honkers land a while back."

Fuzzy and I wanted to stay with Shorty and we wanted to get out of the high grass and be where we could all watch each other's backs. "There sure is a lot of bear sign on these flats," I said to Shorty.

"Go on up there," scowled Shorty. "What's got you boys so jittery? If ya get attacked by a bear, fire your gun off three times and I'll come save ya." He huddled back down under his log and began blowing his goose call.

"Come on, Schoolteacher, we need a goose for Thanksgiving dinner," Fuzzy prompted. But, to be honest, the idea of creeping through that long grass with brown bears all around was making us jumpy. We didn't want to *become* a Thanksgiving Day dinner.

Following the river we found many half eaten salmon carcasses and an old set of bear tracks as big as a man's boot. "You still have that stupid cowbell?" Fuzzy asked. He always made fun of the cowbell that I kept in my pack to scare away bears as I hiked along the trail in Calamity Springs. The townsfolk hated my cowbell and claimed that it woke them up at night. But I'm alive to say that no bear has ever attacked me on my way home from the Calamity Tavern. I retrieved it from my pack.

"Give it good shake now," he implored.

When I shook my cowbell the beaver pond, which was much closer than we might have guessed, erupted in a colossal cacophony of honking. The whole pond came alive with honkers, and a variety of other game birds as well, which all flew up and out through the gap on the opposite side. Fuzzy and I bolted for the pond with our shotguns at the ready but when we arrived at the water's edge there was nothing left to see but a few goose feathers floating among the fresh ripples on the agitated pond. We could hear, above the softly fading honking of a thousand geese, the snorting and cussing from Shorty who was down in the flats throwing himself into a tantrum for inviting us along and for wrecking his fine hunting spot.

The pond was at the tideland's edge and a few scrawny trees circled its borders. After a short while I mentioned to Fuzzy that brown bear don't climb trees well. And so we spent the remainder of the day like a couple of squirrels teetering atop those scrawny bull pines. Late into the afternoon Fuzzy broke the silence, "Schoolteacher," he exclaimed, "I see a bear coming through the grass!"

I looked down in the direction he was frantically pointing. There was the huge, brown hump of a hungry Chichagof bear bouncing through the high grass. It stopped for a moment and must have found our trail for it hunkered down out of our view. Suddenly that gigantic bear hump reappeared and started coming directly toward us!

BOOM, BOOM, BOOM! Fuzzy fired three shot in rapid succession. "I'm not high enough in this little tree!" he said in a quivering voice.

"Me neither," I replied trying to climb just a little bit higher in the skinny bull pine.

Shorty's head appeared above the grass out on the flats. He must have crawled up on a driftwood stump. We could see him searchin' around the flats for the bear and for us. His eyes fell on Fuzzy and me up in our safe perches. "What in tarnation are you fools shootin' at?" he yelled.

"We saw a bear Shorty, an' if I was you I'd get up here right now!"

Shorty must have detected the somber seriousness of the reply because he jumped down off of that stump and came running.

"Oh my God, the bear is right behind you, Shorty!" I hollered.

Again Shorty climbed up on some kind of a snag and his little baseball cap was just visible above the high grass. "Where, is it now?" he screamed.

"It's trailing your every move!" Fuzzy warned.

Again Shorty disappeared from view. We watched in horror as the great hump of that giant bear took off after Shorty.

"Run Shorty, Run!" we called out in a desperate attempt to help our endangered friend. Shorty would, no doubt, soon be another statistic in the Bear Encounters Hall of Fame.

From our high vantage we watched that great lumbering hulk chase our partner. Straight as an arrow they dashed toward our tree stand. As if emerging from a nightmare Shorty broke out of the long grass and onto a sand bar. The giant bear seemed so close behind that it was nearly clinging to his back. Shorty was still a ways off when he slid down into a depression and was lost from our view. I made the sign of the cross thinking I'd never see my little buddy whole again but Shorty was up in a flash and making' a dash to our sanctuary.

He arrived at the base of my tree covered from head to toe in gooey mud. He was panting and red faced, and he danced a wild jig, all the time swearing like a logger. "Gawl Dang It!" he screamed. "Help me get up there." He was jumping up and down trying to grab the lowest branch of my tree. Finally, he wrapped his muddy legs around the trunk and shimmied up like a porcupine. I leaned down, took him by the wrist and ducked as he scampered up and over me and lit in the puny branches overhead.

We looked back toward that mud hole expecting the terrible bear to come roaring out at any time but everything was quiet. There was only the sound of Shorty's heavy panting and the terrified moaning of Fuzzy to break the stillness of the November dusk.

In the cold moonlight we three men clung on for our very lives. Shorty was cussin' the whole night long and askin' Fuzzy an' me questions about the bear. "I never even saw it!" Shorty proclaimed. "Was it really as big as you fellas claim?"

"Oh yes, It was a huge and monstrous bear! We've never seen anything like it."

Every time I tried to change my position the whole tree would sway and threatened to topple over and Shorty would let out a hair-raising scream. As the first light of dawn began to appear in the east Shorty asked, "Do you boys think that we should venture down and have a look? I'm terribly cold and pinched in this tree."

Fuzzy and I would bravely deny ourselves the comforts of terra firma. "Not yet" Fuzzy said. "That bear is more patient for man-meat then you give him credit for." So we stayed shivering up in our roosts until the sun shone on us.

Finally we climbed down out of those trees. With our guns at the ready we crept toward the mud hole where we'd seen Shorty fall. There, in the deep puddle atop the perfect imprint of a small man, was Shorty's huge brown, canvas decoy bag, bulging to the brim with twenty fat, plastic goose decoys. Oddly, there was no trace of the mysterious bear.

"Where're the tracks?" whispered Shorty.

"He must be one very cunning and dangerous bear to cover his tracks so well," I explained academically.

Fuzzy ducked toward the river, and with his fist, pounded some pad marks into the mud. He then stuck his fingers deep into the mud to replicate claw marks. "Here's a fresh track!" he called out while pointing to his creation.

"WHEW-WE!" That was a close one, Boys!" Shorty affirmed.

We walked back to our boats in a strange, communal silence. We had shared a life and death experience and the bonds between men under such circumstances grow strong. Fuzzy and I were in possession of a certainty of purpose that had the effect of clarifying our shared bonds. We knew for certain, that through luck or through divine intervention, we had just barely escaped with our hides. And we knew that if Shorty *ever* found out about our innocent mistake his revenge would be awful.

All the way back to Calamity Springs we told one another about the horrid things that Shorty would do to us if he ever found out why he'd spent the night covered with mud and shivering atop a skinny bull pine in Foggy Flats. We made a solemn pact of silence concerning the matter. That pact has stood firmly all these past thirty years.

Yesterday, I heard that Shorty, who had just turned ninety-three years old, passed away quietly in his bed at the Pioneers Home in Juneau. I called Fuzzy up in Fairbanks and told him the sad news.

"That was a close one," he professed. "School-teacher, I never thought that we could keep the secret for so long. Every time I've spoken to Shorty he brought up the night we were treed by that bear. Thank goodness he never found out that we'd been treed by a bag of goose decoys!"

"Amen! Now he can rest in peace."

"And finally, so can we!"

The Denkeeper

There are creatures below, where men seldom go,
Of a class termed the cephalopods.
They eat and they sleep in the watery deep,
And a few men revere them as gods.

There were three men afloat in an old rubber boat
 Searchin' o're Fredrick Sound,
Attempting to locate the secret lair
Where octopus are found.

Luke hung the anchor down thirty-some feet.
Mac manned the tiller and beer.
Old Jack chuckled nervously sensing his fate
As he fumbled around with his gear.

The anchor struck on a rocky reef,
"We're here, by God," said Jack.
And the three men donned their diving suits,
 And strapped air tanks on their backs.

Fiery eyes to the surface strained
On dark silhouettes of men.
And massive snake-like tentacles
 Receded to their den.

Luke had a flashlight, batteries weak.
Mac had a simple spear.
Old Jack carried nothing but burden unseen,
The weight of incredible fear.

They sunk to five fathoms, where the anchor had
struck,
And the men checked their gages and air.
They signaled "O.K.", and then Jack led the way
Through the dreamscape and into a nightmare.

At thirteen fathoms Luke's light was dull
When they reached an eerie cave.
So no one noticed the bones and skull
That lined their would-be grave.

"Abandon hope, ye who enter here",
Read Dante's Gates to Hell.
Yet two men entered that dark abyss
Where the devilfish might dwell.

Two men entered cautiously
But the diver at their flank,
Loosed the dive knife from his sheath
And rapped it on his tank.

Then the beast shot forth through slimy gore,
Beaconed by a disciple's call.
That eight-armed scourge of sailor lore,
To drop the funeral pall.

In the brief and bloody battle
That in Hell's dark depth's ensued,
Two men became a sacrifice
To a monster strong and shrewd.

When the blood and silt had washed away
And the bubbles ceased to flow,
Old Jack ascended Jesus-rays
To the sun's warm, welcome glow.

And one man laughed from a rubber raft
In Alaska's solitude.
His faith intact by the horrid act
And his strange god's love renewed.

There are creatures below, where men seldom go,
Of a class termed the cephalopods.
They eat and they sleep in the watery deep...
    And a few men revere them as gods.

Hunting Buddha

It was low season in Calamity Springs. The geese and the tourists had all flown south. The bear were in their dens and the tavern was closed. Shorty was out trolling for winter kings and Fuzzy was in his bed with a self-induced headache. I was bored and avoiding my chores when Buddha Bill showed up at my door.

"I saw many blacktail deer on the beach over in Copper Cove. Shall we go hunting, Schoolteacher?" he asked with his strange, lilting Indian accent- a remnant of his childhood. Buddha had been raised in India where his father had been a Methodist Missionary. His offer came as the perfect diversion from a day that would otherwise have been wasted.

"Let's go!" I said, "The laundry and honey bucket can wait another day."

Within the hour we had piled into Buddha's boat and were headed across the inlet to Copper Cove. The weather was cold and foggy and a light snow was drifting across the foredeck as the little diesel chugged its way reliably onward. There, in the heat of the wheelhouse, overpowered by the rich smell of curry, Buddha chatted on and on about growing up in India.

"Did I ever tell you about my Great Tiger Hunt, Schoolteacher?" Buddha always had a tale to tell. "Father had been sent to teach in a small village on the Brahmani River. It was a most peaceful place except for the ferocious tiger that was prowling around and taking the people's goats. The villagers were afraid that a child might become the tiger's next victim so they had hung a goat in a tree, and put a mattress up in the branches, and the men took turns sitting up all night long, waiting with a rifle for the tiger to arrive… to try to steal the goat."

"After awhile, perhaps a week, the men became weary because that tiger would not come to the tree. I begged my father to let me take the rifle and spend a night in the tree. The village men were convinced that the tiger had moved beyond the region and so my father finally agreed. Off I went, shouldering the heavy rifle with my father and our servant, Gishnu guiding me to the tree. When we arrived they helped me to get settled with the rifle, and a flashlight, and my dinner. Then they left me there all alone."

"All night long I waited in the tree. I was hearing scurrying noises through the dry leaves so I would flip on my flashlight and ready the rifle but each time it was always the mongooses, rustling around and pecking at that dead goat. This happened many times. Long about four in the morning I must have drifted off to sleep. When suddenly I awoke with a start and flipped on my flashlight. I looked down, and do you know what? That goat was gone! Then, from behind me I heard a scratching noise and spinning about, I saw the great tiger. He was climbing up that very tree with the heavy goat clamped in his jaws! I roll over on the mattress to get the rifle, but in my haste I roll right out of the tree and I am falling through the black space with my little flashlight pointing up at the tiger with the goat in his mouth. I landed hard on my back and I knocked all the wind out of myself. I didn't know where the gun had fallen and so I close my eyes tight and waited to die. I thought I was a goner, Schoolteacher."

"And suddenly, I feel the great weight of the tiger pouncing on my legs. Now I know that I will soon be dead and I wait for the teeth to crunch down on my bones.... But nothing happens. So I opened one eye and I see that it's just that old dead goat lying across my legs and there is no sign of the tiger. He had run away! I smelled a terrible stench because the goat had been up in that tree for a very long time and when it landed on me it had broken open. I jumped up and I ran as fast as I could back to the village and I was stinking to high heaven! And that was my Great Tiger Hunt."

We anchored up near the old log dump in Copper Cove and set the dinghy over the side. As Buddha paddled us ashore we made a hunting plan. He'd stay low and walk along the beach and I'd go high and skirt the shoreline from above. It was a good plan and if the deer were still nearby, where Bill had spotted them, then we should find them as we drove toward the point.

Bill was right about the deer. I hadn't gone a hundred yards when a small buck stepped in front of me and presented himself. I made a good shot and a clean kill. Bill heard me fire and scurried up in my direction from the beach.

While I dressed my deer, Bill moved up the ridge so he could see down either side as he continued to make his way toward the point. Just a few minutes later I heard two shots boom out from his direction and I left my kill to go see what had happened. As I walked up to Bill he was smiling broadly with his big white teeth nearly aglow.

"I have shot two bucks." Buddha said proudly. "One is right here, and the other," he said as he pointed, "is down in that draw."

Sure enough he had a little two-point down in the draw. "I'll gut that little one down there if you would please take care of this one," he asked.

I busied myself field dressing the larger buck and Bill scurried down the steep-sided ravine and worked on the two-point. When he had dragged it up out of the draw he paused to consider the best way to pack the deer back down to the boat.

"This deer is very small," he noted, "I will carry it over my shoulder if you will please drag the other deer." He asked politely. He then tried to hoist that buck up onto his shoulder but he didn't quite get it high enough. It ended up in the crook of his arm and fell to the ground.

"I had better try this again," he said with determination. This time he practically chucked the little buck into the air. But instead of landing neatly on his shoulder, it landed like a big hat, right on the top of his head. Buddha came to life then, not as a man, but as a deer-man creature. His head had firmly lodged in the chest cavity of the buck and he was dancing around like a mad man trying to get it off.

"Met it moff me. Met it MOFF!!" I could hear his muffled screaming from inside the dancing carcass. I wanted to help him out but I had problems of my own. The paralyzing effects of mirth and hysterical laughter had rendered me useless. Buddha truly looked like a mythical dancing deer. He spun around and around. He hopped up and down. He grunted and lurched. Tears were rolling down my face as I pounded the ground with my fists begging for a reprieve from the hilarious action.

Suddenly a shot rang out. The branch above Bills left antler separated from the tree and came splintering to the ground.

"Get down, Buddha!" I screamed, "Somebody's shootin' at ya."

Just then Buddha Bill caught his foot in a root wad and went tumbling, antlers-over–teacup, back down the steep ravine.

"Don't shoot!" I hollered, "It's Bill! It's Buddha Bill!" I shouted in the direction from which the shot had been fired.

There, before me, rushed Fuzzy, no longer hung over and with his rifle at the ready. "Did ya see him?" he shouted in his deep baritone. "Did ya see my buck go down? I thought I'd missed him, Schoolteacher, but then he went down."

"Put that rifle down, Fuzzy" I hollered, "for you just about killed Buddha Bill!"

Fuzzy and I looked down the ravine just in time to see Buddha eject his head from the stomach cavity of the little buck. He was panting like a dog and his face was crimson red. His dark hair was coated with sticky goo which caused it to spike out every which way. He looked like the devil himself.

"Jesus! Buddha", laughed Fuzzy, "That's a foolish way to dress during huntin' season. You just about got yourself killed!"

"You gentlemen are sworn to secrecy!" Buddha panted. "You shall never mention a word of this to anyone! I will have your solemn oath on this. Yes?"

Well, Fuzzy and I were good to our word, once we quit laughing long enough to give it. And, of course, we never told anyone...until we got back to Calamity Springs.

For the Men at Sea

I ring the bell for the men at sea,
and toast to the fearless few,
Who risk their lives for bounty
on the waters fierce and blue.

From commodore to common hand
they're the bravest lot I know.
That rugged band that shuns the land
 to taste the salty blow.

They're up in the riggin' to lash the main
and in for a horrid trip,
With one hand hold for their mortal soul
and the other for their ship.

They know that calm is fleeting,
and that the gale will surely fly,
And get up from every beating
with a prayer for a gentle sky.

When becalmed at night with the stars aglow
in the vast eternal space,
There's a reverence only seamen know
and it lends 'em special grace.

You're just a speck in the scheme of things
and your life ain't worth a damn,
But you'll fight for it when the riggin' sings
and your crew is in a jam.

Let's drink to their wives and families
who're huddled safe ashore.
Who bravely pray for the safe return
of the men whom they adore.

To the bride whose nightmare fears come true
when the ship and hands are lost,
Whose flowing tears cannot undo
the fate that the sea has tossed.

She'll stand the watch on widow's walks
and stare out to the sea,
And vainly search the lonely docks
 in sad solemnity.

So drink 'em up and grab your gear
for the tide's a comin' in.
And give your sweethearts one last kiss,
and tell your next of kin,

You'll meet in port when we've filled the hold,
if everything goes well.
Then once again we'll spend our gold
and drink to the mighty swell.

We'll tip a glass to the men with brass,
to the souls who're only free,
When we're far from shore and we rise before
 the power of the sea.

So ring the bell for the men at sea,
and toast to the fearless few,
Who risk their lives for bounty
on the waters fierce and blue.

Old Blue

It was just a little squirrel as I think back at it now, but it drove me half insane until I finally learned to accept the things in life that I could never change. Sciuridea, as a species, are generally well tolerated by us humans. Their large eyes and furry tails are considered to be cute by most standards. But on certain occasion they can become more than just a mere nuisance, and to a man with personal space issues, coupled with the dread *cabin fever*, they can become an outright nightmare.

Life in Calamity Springs was what most folks would generously call "laid back", but like most communities we had our problems, and toward the end of an especially long, cold winter the seventy-one human residences had succumbed to a strange psychological phenomenon commonly referred to as 'cabin fever.' I, being human myself, was no exception.

Some of the most common causes of the disorder were lack of sunlight and the close proximity of the cabins and shanties; these structures having been laid out as if the town fathers felt that with a thousand square miles of wilderness in every direction we should be stacked like cordwood along the one mile trail which served as the main drag. This closeness, I believe, was designed to give the inhabitants a sense of security and community. Invariably it becomes a lingering source of aggravation.

Imagine, if you can, being able to hear all of the minute variations in your neighbors snoring. And further imagine having young newlyweds as neighbors. There is no pillow thick enough, when folded against a bachelor's ear, to drown out the low guttural moans of a frolicking couple; no shade is dark enough to cast an opaque shadow on the haunting visions which assault his lonely temporal lobes.

This brings me to another powerful cause for the disorder; the low number of available females as compared to the high number of needy males. The ratio being completely lopsided to the tune of about twenty guys to every gal.

The seasonal closure of the Calamity Tavern also caused some residents to either exhibit a smug, holier-than-thou attitude, or a shaking frustration, depending on their personal viewpoints regarding prohibition and the evils of intoxicating libation.

All of these torments affected the denizens of Calamity Springs, and each to varying degrees depending on individual weaknesses. The overall health of the community was greatly affected. By the end of a cold and slushy March, when springtime seemed but a distant and cruel memory unwilling to show her glorious and voluptuous attributes, the whole village seemed to be cursed and erupted in craziness.

So as to give you, dear reader, some inkling of the strange effusions which were but the outward signs of the afflictions from that wintery plague, I have set down an incomplete inventory of just a few shenanigans which occurred within a brief period prior to the spring thaw:

February 12: The construction crew who were building the inn that was connected to the Calamity Tavern opened a secret bar. It was complete with a little sliding peep hole so they could see who was wanting to come in to gamble and buy the booze which they had borrowed from the stocks of The Tavern.

February 15: Someone tried to burn down the mayor's house. Thankfully, only the front deck got a bit scorched before the town fireman said he "heard smoke" and deputized all the men and women in the secret bar to help him put it out.

February 23: One of the crab boats from Seattle mysteriously caught fire and burned all the way to its waterline. I heard later that it was very well insured.

March 3: The construction crew decided that it would be easier just to open up The Tavern and simply replace the stock they drank up to keep it replenished. Word somehow got out and the owners came in from Juneau and fired everyone on the spot. They all were rehired within a week as they were all locals and the only carpenters within two hundred miles.

March 14: The president of the school board, Mrs. Burley, and the village public safety officer's wife got plastered on homemade blueberry wine and ran down the trail as naked as jaybirds. They were freezin' more than their toes off when they were finally corralled by their husbands and carried like potato sacks, kicking and laughing down the road and home to bed. They both laid low for quite some time after that. The village gossips had themselves a heyday.

March 28: Some mischievous fellow changed all of the women's hours at the public bathhouse for which Calamity Springs is so well known. The men's and women's times were changed to overlap, which caused a huge uproar when a group of elderly ladies disrobed in the dressing room and then entered the steamy bath. Softly at first, then gaining in volume, there could be heard, transmitting below the soft twitterings of feminine discourse, a deep and vibrant baritone.

Emerging through the thick fog of steam, Max Longhammer appeared. He was naked and completely covered in soap, from his thick mane and heavy beard to the tops of his size 16 double E feet. "What are you women doing in the men's bath?" he bellowed.

Agnus Bigalow was so flabbergasted by the sight of the huge man that in her haste to cover herself and depart, she slipped on the wet floor and would have taken a nasty fall if Longhammer hadn't reached out to save her. But as she was struggling to regain her feet she grabbed hold of his… manhood. She was falling and it hung there like a rope. Maxwell screamed. Agnus screamed. All eight of the ladies screamed.

They ran out of the echoing bathhouse, still naked, into the bright March sunshine and onto the snowy trail. Once outside, the disoriented grannys flew headlong into me and my class of thirteen year old boys headed down to the village library on an academic outing. I have since learned, sadly, that some sights once seen, can never be unseen.

Because of all of the aforementioned factors; please allow me to recapitulate those factors: 1.) reduced daylight hours, 2.) loneliness, 3.) nothin' to do, and 4.) our close proximity, the citizens of Calamity Springs became adversely affected in the neighborhood of our mental health. But the straw that broke the camel's back, at least for me, was a little, gray pine squirrel. . .

*   *   *

One afternoon after a hard and frustrating day of trying to fill the brains of the village children with lasting knowledge, I arrived at home to find a little gray squirrel perched atop my cabin door. My first reaction was a feeling of camaraderie. We were two like souls, lonely and chattering our frustrations to a cruel and heartless world. And so I considered the little fella my new companion, although at times, he seemed to be scolding me with an obnoxious cheeck-teeck-cheecking noise that grated on my already fragile nerves.

As time passed the squirrel became more and more bold. It would drop sticks and pinecones on my head whenever I ventured outside. Then, one day in late March, it decided to move in with me.

The first time he actually came into my territory was late one night when I had stumbled down from the sleeping loft to relieve myself in the honey bucket out in the wannigan. As I sat quietly in the dark, enclosed porch, my pajamas around my ankles, and my mind wrapped around itself, something big and hairy ran across my cold, bare feet.

Visions of giant Norwegian rats came at once into my mind and I jumped up screaming like a child. I burst through the door and back into the cabin proper, my pants still down and my business still unfinished.

I lit the oil lamp and armed myself with my Remington 870 pump action 12 gauge shotgun. I then hobbled back out to the wannigan. I opened the door nervously and set about making a careful search. I cautiously moved aside the tools, and then the buckets, and the axes. Soon, the number of hiding places was diminished to a point that I was certain to discover the source of my dread behind the last, lonely shovel occupying the darkest corner of the shed.

I leaned forward holding out the kerosene lantern with one hand and gripping the shotgun with the other. With my thumb, I clicked the safety to off. There are many strange and mysterious stories of beasts that lurk in the primordial forests and waters in southeast Alaska; The Kooshnikaw, the Sasquatch, the Otter-man and others. All of these ghouls congregated in my mind there in the dark and cold wannigan.

Suddenly, something terrible jumped down out of the rafters and dug it's sickening claws into the flesh of my back through the thin t-shirt. The shotgun fired a deafening blast and I let out a cry that must have awakened the dead. From the top of my head a violent tremor took hold of me and continued to grow until it literally shook my whole being to its core. Scampering across my back from one shoulder to another and back again, the horrific beast finally bolted out the door allowing me just the briefest glimpse of its grotesque and bushy tail in the blue moonlight.

I spent the remainder of the night boiling water on the stove and repeatedly washing away the creepy bugs and fleas that I vividly imagined to be infesting my body.

The very next day the brash beast bravely came into my cabin. I was lying on the couch reading a Louie L'Amour novel when the intruder streaked overhead. It scampered from one beam to the next, chattering incessantly before finally exiting out through a small hole on the other side of the cabin. He had invaded my domain and I decided then and there that the consequences should be severe.

I went up to the sleeping loft and grabbed up my twenty-two caliber rifle. I then went outside resolutely, to track down and kill the little varmint.

I was sneaking around the cabin, when my neighbor, Albert, who had been down to the beach emptying his honey bucket, spied me and grew alarmed by my armed and angry attitude.

"Whatcha up to, Schoolteacher?" he hollered while eyeing me suspiciously.

I told him the story of the terrible rodent. Albert had been awakened the previous night by a horrific scream and the sound of gunfire emanating from the direction of my cabin and he offered little in the way of solace to temper my tale of woe.

Instead, he embarked on one of his usual, strangely appropriate dissertations. "The earliest fossil record of a squirrel is from thirty-five million years ago," he informed me. "You go back far enough, Schoolteacher, and you can just bet that you and that varmint have common kin. And you should note too, that they have thumbs, whether that's a curse or a blessing I don't know for sure, but it seems you might want to give that little fella a chance to live and be happy seein' how destiny has somehow drawn you two together on an intersecting course."

"Thumbs?" I wondered. I looked up on my roof and spied the creature of my torment. It was spinning a pinecone deftly in its paws. I studied harder and focused my eyes on those little claws. Sure enough, the devil had thumbs!

Now, havin' thumbs makes a difference on how a critter ought to be treated. You and I have thumbs and some scientists believe that it is that very trait which led to our use of tools and the enlargement of our brains. (Although some folks who don't have much in the way of brains, have retained a fine pair of opposable thumbs.)

Albert then informed me that he happened to be in possession of a 'Have-a-Heart' live trap which he had brought in from Juneau to rid himself of a similar nuisance. His idea to catch it seemed like a good one to me. That old squirrel, having thumbs like mine, and the idea that the two of us were likely derived of a common ancestor had softened my resolve.

Albert and I dusted off the old, rusty trap and oiled the mechanism which attached the bait tray to a spring-loaded door. We then baited the trap with some Beer Nuts from his larder. I climbed up on a ladder and placed the trap on the eaves above the gutter where the little devil had often sat and scolded me.

He was a smart and wily little fiend and somehow he emptied the trap of its delicious contents three times before, on the third day, I finally hair triggered the device and it slammed shut on the rascal.

Now I had the demon but was unsure of what to with him. Albert's advice was to haul him two miles down the trail to the other side of the boat harbor and let him go in the woods there.

So it was that on April the first we set off on the relocation mission. I have to tell you that I was none too gentle when I finally opened the cage and shook the weasel out.

Hiking back homeward, I felt content in the knowledge that things had ended so peacefully. I was glad that I hadn't killed the little bugger and was pleased that I'd have my cabin to myself.

Albert and I were congratulating ourselves for a job well done when we arrived back at the cabin. But there, standing angrily on the ridge cap with his little fists resting on his hips like an old woman, was the angry little gremlin. He was furiously scolding and chattering like all get out at Albert and me.

"That absolutely cannot be the same squirrel," Albert exclaimed while scratching his head.

"How could he have beaten us home?" I wondered aloud.

"You must have two squirrels, Schoolteacher," Albert proclaimed unconvincingly.

There was but one way the story could end now and I went in to fetch my gun. But while I was in the cabin Albert was busy reloading the trap. When I came back outside he tried to convince me that this new squirrel was the mate to the one we had just relocated, and that, in the name of love, we should catch this one as well and send her off to rejoin her husband.

Because there really wasn't much to do in Calamity Springs at that time of year to entertain a person, I finally relented, with one condition. I was absolutely convinced that there was only one squirrel and that if we could catch this one again, I would somehow mark him and see if he ever returned to torment me.

Albert agreed to my little experiment and we made a small wager as to the outcome.

It took two days of replenishing the Beer Nut bait before I finally caught the other squirrel. Before I ran over to tell Albert, I located a can of blue spray paint and went to work on my squirrel. When I was finally satisfied with my handiwork, I had a beautiful blue-tailed squirrel.

Once more we took off for the harbor. We released the squirrel in the same area as before, then we high-tailed it back to my cabin in Calamity Springs. There was no sign that we were being followed as we were stealthy men; mere shadows drifting unseen through a primordial forest. Before we got back to my cabin we could hear a terrible commotion. There, on the peak of my roof, was the angriest blue-tailed squirrel I'd ever seen, and would ever hope to see.

This time Albert waited patiently as I went in and loaded my gun.

When I emerged from the cabin, I traipsed up the hill behind so I could get a clear shot of the varmint without risking shooting a hole in the cabin's roof.

As he hunched up on the ridge cap I put the rifle to my shoulder and had him centered in my sights. He looked really cute, sitting on his haunches and nibbling on a pinecone, and the thought of being rid of him was overcome by a kind of transcendental understanding. Here was a magnificent, thumbed creature. He was alive just like me. He ate and slept and worried about things. He worked hard to fill a larder and must have been successful too, as he was very healthy looking despite his azure pelt.

My resolve softened once again and I wondered if we could ever live together in harmony. I slid the safety on and climbed down to the front of the cabin.

"Change your mind, Schoolteacher?" Albert smiled.

"We came to an understanding," I replied.

The following week the sun came out brightly and warmed the earth. Springtime and flowers and some degree of normalcy returned to Calamity Springs. Such is the way of things in the wilderness, enemies become friends and winter turns to spring.

Like the melting snows on the mountaintops so was my agitation and cabin fever melting away.

It turns out that Old Blue, as I came to call her, was a female and pregnant to boot. She set up a nest in the walls of our living area and proceeded to have a nice batch of squirrelets. We decided to end our feud and became happy roommates. I would feed them a mess of peanuts every morning before I went off to work and never did tire of their crazy acrobatic antics as they flew from one beam to another across the ceiling of my cabin.

To this day I feel a special kinship with squirrels; a kinship especially strong on such occasion as I am enjoying a glass of fine sherry wine. Sherry wine will always remind me of the tasty bottle that I won in my little wager with Albert. And when I'm drinking a nice glass of fine sherry wine… I proudly use my thumbs.

BONFIRES

We danced about
The fires of youth.
Fearless and wild,
Searing our scars.
Flying the sparks
Of creative ideals
Aloft in smoky
Self-indulgence.

We laughed and cried,
And fought unharmed.
We drank good scotch,
(As gentlemen might)
Arm in arm and
Softly whiskered.

We turned our backs
To the dark of age.
Our breath and song
Became the air,
Was forged in life.
And sought the truth
In the intimate earth,
And the flickering flames.

Then wandering out,
One by one,
Away from the warmth.
We tempered our hearts
In the oily night.
We stood our ground
Professed our truths
Fought tooth and nail
Grew old
Transformed by age
To ancient relics.

We tumbled and cracked
Were shattered and scraped
Pounded and polished
In the churning, roaring
Waves of time.

The Index Card

When a man decides that it's his time to settle down, and sets out to find the woman who will be his mate for life, all semblance of rational thought is thrown to the wind. He evolves into a creature unrecognizable to those whom he had known prior to his epiphany. It's a transformation, from the feminine view, devoutly to be wished. He washes more thoroughly, shaves more closely, and brushes harder. He swears less, dresses better, and takes in his drink with more moderation. His manners become impeccable. As for the demeanor of his speech, where once there were only rigid facts and concrete knowledge, there is supplanted in his mouth a flowery discourse, and to those most afflicted, even a hint of poetry. It's a time when life-long and staunch Republicans might see the wisdom of a liberal Democrat, or an atheist discovers God.

The only really troubling thing about this transformation is that it's a sham, a flim-flam, and a con. Once the hunt is over the hunter reverts back to his former self and, to the dismay of the captured prey, becomes a man once again with all of his human frailties revealed.

I can't proclaim that these deceptions are voluntary. They are not. Mother Nature wants her creatures to procreate and multiply, and without such trickery the human species might have succumbed to the same fate of the dodo bird. Nature, though sweet, can also exhibit exquisite cruelty.

The transfiguration of the male is trivial as compared to the metamorphosis of the female, who herself is influenced, nay, *compelled* by the urgent and inconsolable nesting mandate. It is the call of the wild, beckoning her to dye the hair and girdle the waist, to moisturize and blush the cheek, to uplift and amplify the chest, or tighten and minimize the thigh, to paint the lips, extend the lash, and fast for days on end so she can fit into clothes which cause her physical pain and discomfort. It is the most profound and ribald deception in all of the animal kingdom.

She knows how to use each of the male's senses against him. He smells the wafting perfume on her neck, sees the slightly revealing cleaving of her rising breast, feels the soft, warm touch of her breath in his ear, and suddenly, the trap falls, "Snap!"

Besides the astounding physical modifications a female might promote as her true figure, there are other, more subtle ruses which she will use to mollify a mate. There is the reverence she displays in reaction to his worldly revelations. He is wise, and strong, and knowledgeable, she professes, her voice never climbing a decibel higher than that of a songbird. And when she speaks, her words are soft and pleasant, and always full of encouragement and praise.

Neither sex can be trusted to display their true characters while the courtship display in being acted out. Both are equally guilty of deception. Neither can be blamed, for nature and genetics are the predominant factors which are simply conniving to achieve a unity resulting in the propagation of the species. However, despite the innocence of the mating pair, certain misconceptions are being advertised as truths and the disparity will eventually be revealed.

Successful realization of a lifelong relationship is accomplished by the ability of both parties to accept the fact that these exaggerations were put forth for a greater good. You continue to live with that special person, who is inevitably revealed as a common and ordinary soul, complete with flaws, both physical and emotional. You know that you've been a victim of misrepresentations. Marriage is the acceptance of the revelation that one's been lied to, and the ability to take it on the chin. So you shake it off and get on with your life, this is what makes for an enduring relationship. This is the institution of marriage, *the fragile compromise.*

There came a time in my own life when finding a mate became my obsession. I always thought that this type of nesting instinct was only a feminine phenomenon, but that was before it happened to me. It was as if I'd caught a disease of some kind. I couldn't sleep, food lost its flavor, and life in general took on a more primordial attitude. Hunting and gathering were not enough.

I needed a mate but, at the same time, dating took on a fiercer aspect. Small talk with women ended up like interrogations about their childhood. I asked them stupid questions like whether or not they loved their families or what they thought about having kids. I said things like, "Maybe we should take things slowly," and, "There are more important things in a relationship than sex." I started to feel that I was cursed.

It all began when I was approaching thirty years of age and living in Calamity Springs, a remote Alaskan village with very few marriageable females. A strange course of events led me to love, and then to marriage, and eventually to fatherhood and beyond. The one thing that I know for sure is that I had little, if anything, to do with the direction in which my life went. I was a hostage on the express train of life, and a captive of the amazing and often surreal ways of a mystical fate.

As a matter of fact, it was fate and the Baptists who had a marked impact on my search for love. I was the innocent victim of a spell cast by an itinerant preacher. You see, when a minister of the Baptist church came to town on his monthly pilgrimage to convert and absolve sinners, I attended the church meeting.

It was another dull Wednesday evening when Pastor Pete arrived in his Piper Cub to hold a revival at the Calamity Hall, and I being bored to tears, had no choice but to attend. I was neither a Baptist nor an especially religious man, but entertainment is a relative thing, and you'll never find any if don't look for it. It's like fishin'; you can't catch a fish if your line's not wet. So that cold and rainy night I got my rubber clothes on and trudged down the trail to the church meeting, to everlasting salvation, and to a new and very different life. Had I not attended that evening service my life might have been very, very different.

The service itself was a basic affair. Six of us sinners sat on metal folding chairs. We sang the songs and recited the necessary recitations to guarantee the forgiveness of our sins and entry into the Pearly Gates. At the end of the service, over coffee and cookies, Pastor Pete asked me how I was enjoying my life in the bush, to which I replied that overall, things were just wonderful. Then, in an offhand remark, I stated my strong and growing desire for female companionship. To be clear, I think I said *meaningful* female companionship, after all he was a preacher and I didn't want to seem lecherous. And *meaningful* really was what I thought I wanted.

"Well then," Pete exclaimed, "this is a job for the Lord. Schoolteacher, I want you to take this three by five index card and write down what it is you are looking for in a woman. I'll take it back to my congregation in Juneau and we'll all pray for you. Schoolteacher, don't be surprised that, if in the next few weeks, your future wife steps up to you and the work of the Lord will be made flesh." And then as if to prove his snake-potion claims, he pointed to his wife and proclaimed, "That's how I met my Little Bertie". Bertha looked up from the piano bench where she'd been playing hymns all evening and flashed a big smile. I noticed that she was anything but little. And wondered what Pete had written on *his* index card.

Strange notions came into my head at that moment. I often wonder what exciting and wonderful attributes I might have requested on that little white card if I'd really thought that there was any truth to it. I must tell you that it is a curious feeling when one imagines that a wish could be granted. I felt that within my hand was the power to ask for anything I wanted. My head spun with unusual fantasies before I realized that another session of sin forgiving might be necessary if I didn't redirect my chain of thought. In front of me stood a man of the cloth and so, with some reserve, I filled out the little card. In a loose and illegible scrawl I asked the Lord to procure for me a woman with a pretty face, a slender waist, long legs, and a good sense of humor. It may seem like shallow criteria, but it was the best I could do on short notice, and I was still unconvinced of the legitimacy of the endeavor.

Great Alaskan Shorts

Two weeks to the day had passed when Scruffy and I made our weekly pilgrimage to the Alaska ferry dock to check for any pretty, young women getting off. I had told Scruffy about my index card and he, in turn, had blabbed about it to all of the people in Calamity Springs. Everyone in the village offered advice and encouragement. Old ladies slipped me the phone numbers of their nieces, and groups of men would follow me to the float-plane dock and ferry terminal shouting words of encouragement.

Scruffy and I had met every floatplane and ferry since the fateful prayer meeting and I was about to give up all hope when, suddenly, I was astounded to see the lady of my index card walking up the gangway from the Alaska ferry *Taku* with a group of women. When I saw her, I was a goner and could see by her long legs and flashing smile that my prayers had been answered. Scruffy and I both became religious converts right there on the spot.

Comforted by a gang of well-wishers we followed the girls to Rosie's Blue Moon Café where I uncustomarily, rang the bell to buy drinks for the house. Eventually, I began to make small talk with the woman. Little did I know that she too was look-

Page 73

ing for a life mate and had already assumed the deceptive demeanor of a woman enthralled with the amazing feats and accomplishments of such an interesting man as myself.

In Alaska there are a lot of single men but, no offense intended, they are a lot of men like Scruffy and Shorty. They're 'the breed of men who won't give in' as the great poet Robert Service would say. Scruffy *had* given in four times and gone through four ugly divorces, two to the same woman. Shorty on the other hand had never given in and never would. He eventually died a happy bachelor up in Fairbanks at the Pioneers home. I, however, was of the breed of men who must give in. My fall was swift and complete. My transition absolute.

I didn't see hide nor hair of that woman for two months. But then, on my way to Murray Pacific in Sitka to buy boat paint, there she was on the Ferry *Taku*. We chatted for hours and I met her mother who was there on vacation. The two had booked a trip to Sitka to explore southeast Alaska. We kissed in Angoon under a full moon and thus began the year of courtship. I cleaned up my act and would write her poems about love and life. I changed my sheets and generally became a gentleman.

Fanny lived in Juneau and I in Calamity Springs and so our meetings were clandestine weekends in one of the two places. One morning, after an exceptionally pleasant night, I was dressed in a clean robe and slippers and drinking good coffee, freshly brewed by *my girlfriend*, when I said something that changed the course of my life forever. The actual words escape my recollection now, but must have been transmitted in their underlying tone as the inkling of an idea, an offer, it seems, for Fanny to give up her good job and her nice apartment in Juneau, and move to Calamity Springs to be my live-in girlfriend.

One night a few weeks after that vague conversation I was sitting at the Calamity Tavern when Shorty burst in the door.

"Schoolteacher!" he cried, "You better get outside right now 'cause there's a woman pulling a cart down the trail. She's angry, Schoolteacher, and she's a lookin' fer ya."

"Me?" I asked. "Now what could that be about?"

A group of my pals followed me out of the Tavern and sure enough there in the soft moonlit night was Fanny. She was panting hard and pulling like a sled dog harnessed to a heavy cart with big steel wheels. On top of the cart, piled to the stars was a load of girly things and personal belongings crammed into a huge contraption with drawers full of drawers and with a half-closet built right into the top.

Fanny seemed upset that I had not only forgotten to meet the ferry, but had seemed to obliterate any memory of my life changing invitation. And so, among the jeering jabs from a throng of masculine onlookers, I did what any descent man would do, I inscripted volunteers. We shoved and lugged that big Armoire up the steep steps and into my cabin. Once there, with a whole lot of gruntin', and some cussin', we fought her armoire all the way up the ladder and into my sleeping loft. From that day forth it was *our* sleeping loft.

She immediately set to work redecorating the cabin with an endless treasure-trove of nick-knacks and curios, all spit out from that limitless and mysterious armoire. She even put a soft, pink carpet around the honey bucket out in the wannigan. Finally, she hung her Catholic crucifix above the cabin door and proclaimed that it was now a livable abode. I often imagine that the Lord Almighty has a strange and mighty sense of humor, especially where that Baptist and the Catholics are concerned.

So, that is how it is, the hunter becomes the hunted. I'd like to tell you that I was in no way disturbed by this strange turn of events, but I have to admit that I was perplexed and mystified by the scene.

At the time, my students were rehearsing a school play called 'The Monkey's Paw' a story in which, through a mysterious power, folks were granted wishes. The one that came to mind most powerfully was the scene in which an elderly couple wished that their dead son would come back to them. Sure enough he did, but he was still as dead as a doorknob, a worm-eaten zombie haunting their quaint cottage. The theme was surely that old adage, 'Be careful what you wish for'. I wondered aloud, "Was my Baptist index card like the proverbial Monkey's Paw?"

What was I going to do now that the index card had fulfilled its promise? How would my life change? Was I ready for such a sweeping redirection of my bachelor ways? Prepared, I was not.

I was immediately delegated the chores of a manservant. The first big challenge was the removal of all the mice and the nice family of squirrels that I had recently become accustomed to. That alone proved to be an ongoing battle. I would come home from school and find Fanny upstairs perched atop her armoire. She'd be screaming that mice had run across her feet. From below, in the kitchen area, I would stamp my feet several times and assure her that I had killed a half dozen or so of the varmints. Then I'd tell her that I was going to practice my taxidermy and make a pair of gloves out of there little hides, complete with their little tails, and she would scream again that she didn't want anything to do with dead mice, and that I was to get their carcasses out of the cabin, and pronto.

I never really killed any of the mice and the squirrels left of their own accord, on account of all the commotion. The best thing to come out of those charades was that I had her undying love and thanks for exterminating the beasts. And the rewards were wonderful to behold!

I was a man in love and I would do whatever it took to procure happiness and to ensure the heartfelt devotion of my life.

Six months later we were married. It was a tag-team affair conducted by a bashful Bishop and a boastful Baptist in the Calamity chapel.

Puzzles

You hold and turn perplexing shapes to fit the myriad of choices in your lives; the infinite array of pleasures and of sins, to spin and ponder to discern, or be content to recognize. Then flip one over and find reference to a subtle shape much different than the solid matched experience held before. And test the bulbous edge of maleness to an accepting female form, but overlook the imperfections, as a balance is implied to verify the norm. You study every attribute until it seems the problem's solved, but lacking precognition you won't know if it's resolved. For each arrangement has a consequence, each decision, an effect. So you fit the pieces cautiously, and reconsider which temptations to reject. Then waver to commit, but finally press and snap to frame the interlocking symbols never leaving you the same. Each enduring placement causing everything to change; a conscious move thus binding and misshaping the intent, and locking one to each, the whole and all the parts to rearrange. And when the final piece is set, the puzzle of a life is done. To flaunt or curse the finished self, and what it has become. A life that's pieced together without providential rules, but the deeds of ancient heroes and prophetic parables, loosely bound to give protection from the influence of fools. Then you'll sense the great dilemma that each dying soul must face. To be forged in life's transgressions and distorted imperfections, yet in the end your invocations plead for grace. Fit carefully the shapes of your free will … imperfect race.

The Man Who Knew Women

There once was a man who knew everything that there was to know about women. He was a confirmed bachelor and a hermit who resided in a small cabin on the outskirts of Calamity Springs. I was his pupil.

Slim Osborne was a tall and angular man in his mid-seventies. He was clean shaven with a mop of thick gray hair that framed his deeply lined and strangely handsome face. We had become close friends when he'd asked me to help him drag a buck off the top of Big Baldy Mountain during the fall of my first year of teaching at the Calamity Springs School. Slim always wore fresh woolies and long johns even during the warmer months, which I figured was a result of his poor circulation. His kitchen window sill looked like a pharmacy, piled high with a multitude of amber colored pill bottles containing the medications that he needed to take for his bad ticker.

He was the most self-sufficient person I'd ever met. Besides putting up venison, salmon, shrimp and crab, he also worked a small vegetable garden and he even had a little window box where he grew fresh herbs to add to his famous soups and stews. He collected blueberries and huckleberries in August which he made into sweet wine and delicious jams. His modest cabin was always tidy and had the odd distinction of being the only cabin in Calamity Inlet with hot running water. Slim had installed a coil system through his stove that heated water. He even had a flush toilet and a bathtub. Everyone else, that I knew, bathed at the Calamity Springs public bathhouse.

One afternoon, as he puttered around his neat little kitchen, he began to explain the mysteries of women to me. "Women ain't like you." he said. "If you've made up your mind to marry one of 'em, then there's a few thing you ought to know, Schoolteacher. The first thing to keep in mind is that you aren't in charge, they are." He sat down across from me at the little table. His dark eyes seemed to burn into me and I got the strange feeling that he could read my mind.

"Oh, she'll probably let you go on thinkin' that it's you who's the boss, but it won't be so. Take old Farley and Emma, I asked him on his fiftieth anniversary if he could tell me his secret to a long and happy marriage." Slim got up to fill my coffee mug and offered me a slice of huckleberry pie. It was still warm.

"Farley told me that he and Em had made an arrangement right off the bat. She would take care of all the day to day decisions in their lives, and he would be asked to step in and make the really big ones. So I asked him, 'Farley, in fifty years of marriage how many big decisions did you end up getting stuck with?' and do you know what, Schoolteacher? Farley thought about that question for a long time, and then he looked up at me, all befuddled-like, and admitted that he guessed that there hadn't been any; because he couldn't think of a one. That's what you have to look forward to, my boy."

"That doesn't sound so bad," I said meekly.

"Don't be a dumbass, this is serious business. Marriage is nothin' but sanctified slavery, Schoolteacher, and you're the one who'll be wearin' the shackles."

"But I love her Slim, and I've already sown all my wild oats. I'm thirty years old and it's time for me to settle down and maybe even have a family."

"Speakin' of families", Slim continued, "What do know about hers?"

"I don't know. They seem like nice folks."

"You've got to do some research, Boy. Find out if her parents were divorced. Find out if she loves her mother or if she hasn't spoken to a sibling because of some old squabble. These are important questions, Schoolteacher. They tell you a lot about her values and how she thinks. Women aren't like used cars you know. You don't buy a clunker thinkin' that you can fix it up nice once you get it home. What you get… is what you get."

I walked out into the rain feeling less certain that I was cut out for marriage. Fanny wasn't a clunker, I assured myself, but as I made the hike back to Calamity Springs, I decided that Slim was right. I had some research to do.

A few days later I ran into Slim at the Pioneers Hall where Fanny was cooking for the old timers. I had so much to tell him, but I felt uncomfortable with Fanny always fluttering about and lookin' over my shoulder. Slim seemed to sense that I needed to talk, so we set up a date for a fishing expedition. The cohos were running and Slim always needed someone to go out with on account of his bad heart.

The next morning at six a.m. I was at his cabin to help haul gear down to his skiff. As Slim filled a thermos with coffee and wrapped up a few sandwiches, I was just burstin' to tell him the news. "She's got a nice family," I blurted. "Her parents have never been divorced and she gets along well with all four of her brothers and sisters. In fact, they're all comin' up her for our wedding in November."

"So you've been doin' your homework, Schoolteacher, that's good, "Slim seemed impressed. "And I'll just bet that she was grateful that you were so curious about her past."

I hadn't really thought about it, but Slim had hit the nail on the head. "Yes sir," I said, "she talked on and on about herself."

"Women love it when you ask about them. They're creatures of the heart you know. And they love to talk. That's one thing you're gonna have to get used to."

"I don't mind," I said. "I like listenin' to her."

"Sure you do," he said, but he sounded unconvinced.

As we sat together in the skiff surrounded by a thick fog and moochin' for coho, Slim talked on and on about the fish he'd taken from the deep waters below the rocky ledge out near the mouth of Calamity Inlet. Then we both got kind of quiet and thoughtful. Fishin' with a friend in the fog is a great way to pass the time. Eventually Slim asked me, "So Schoolteacher, how many kids are you two going to have?"

"I don't know, maybe one or two, in a couple of years, we'll see."

"Try four or five", was his quick response, "and expect the first to arrive within the year."

"No way!" I replied. Just then I had a great tug on my line and for the next ten minutes or so we busied ourselves getting the first coho in the boat. It was a nice fish, maybe ten pounds and bright silver.

After a brief celebration Slim continued right where he'd left off. He said with gravity. "Have you even discussed this with the little woman?"

"What?"

"Kids."

"Well, not exactly," I admitted, "But we're both conscientious about over population."

"Fanny is Catholic, isn't she? And she comes from a big family herself, you told me that. And how old is she now? About thirty, right?"

"She's only twenty eight," I said, trying to sound indignant.

The rest of the morning was consumed by some pretty good fishin' with no more talk about kids. Slim could see that he'd left me confused and dropped the subject.

We headed back to Calamity about noon and Slim asked if I would help him with getting the catch into canning jars. "The canning is as much fun as the catching," he said. "When the fish are cleaned, and filleted, and put up in jars to be enjoyed all winter long, it's a lot like marriage, Schoolteacher," he said with a malicious twinkle in his eye, "once the honeymoon is over."

"How many fish did we get today, Teach?" he asked as he brought the pot of canning jars to a roiling boil.

"Well, you know as well as I do that I caught four and you got three. But that one hen you brought in was the biggest of the bunch."

"Women don't keep score like men do," he said. "They're in it for the socializing more than anything and they don't care who catches more. What's more, women are often better fishermen than men. Fill those jars with chunks of meat right up to here," he demonstrated, "Then add a spoonful of these spices and but 'em on this rack."

"Why's that?" I asked. It felt good to stand in his warm kitchen and have a specific job to do. All the same he kept a watchful eye on how I filled the jars.

"Because they don't mind asking questions and they don't act like they know everything. They're not afraid of looking ignorant. Why, a woman can walk right up to one of them high-liners and ask them where to fish and what bait to use, and he'll just tell her straight out. Yes sir, if you want to catch more fish, get that soon-to-be-bride of yours interested. You'll do well."

"So women make great spies", I said and I considered what Slim was saying. It sounded good to me. I remembered the time when I'd asked my friend Shorty where he'd caught a nice mess of kings, he hooked his finger into the side of his mouth and he said, "Right dere." I never asked again.

"When a man tells another man a story, that guy's not listening. He's too busy trying to think of his own story; one that he thinks can top his friends' tale. But when a woman tells another woman a story, she'll listen intently and ask for more details if something's unclear. She'll try to put herself in that other woman's shoes. She wants to feel what her friend felt and learn from it. Oh sure, often times it's just idle gossip, but those stories are important to a woman and they're passed down from one generation to the next. It's how they learn so much without always havin' to end up in a pickle first."

"Are all women like that?" I asked.

"No, not all, there are a few that are more like you and me, but I don't imagine that your Fanny is one of 'em. They're the ones who become CEO's or get into politics."

That night I slept fitfully and had a rare nightmare. Fanny was downstairs puttering over the stove. Water was boiling in a big pot and she stood over it humming. Parts of me were laid out on the kitchen table and she picked up globs of them and slid them into quart jars, added some spices, put them on a rack, then lowered them into the boiling pot. "The catching is fun, but the canning is sweeter. These jars will be a great treat to take down off the shelf and consume in the winter of my life," she sang. I awoke with a start.

The next day I wasn't my jolly self at school. The kids were all restless from the weekend and I was in a grumpy mood. It was the first of my 'cold feet' moments. Later that week, Fanny and I had our first fight.

I'd bumped into Shorty outside The Calamity Tavern on my way home from school and we went in together. Fuzzy was already there, and the three of us started gabbin' about diesel engines, and then fishin', and then Fuzzy told us that he had seen a big buck over near Copper Bay. Anyway, one thing led to another and Shorty was in one of his very rare good moods and was buying the drinks. The next thing I knew it was about eight o'clock and I was getting' ready to shove off when Fanny came through the door as mad as a hornet.

"Is this where you've been all night?" she asked. "I don't think you're very considerate. I've been home worried sick about you. There are bears about... I made you a nice venison roast with twice baked potatoes, the way you like 'em, and now it's all gone cold. We need to talk!" she said. And before I could explain, she spun around, kicked open the tavern door and vanished into the darkness.

"You're in big trouble now, Schoolteacher," Shorty slurred. And he was right.

There was nothin' I could say or do to pacify my love. I tried to talk some sense into her but, for the first time since I'd known her, she didn't seem to want to talk. "It's no big deal," I explained. "I was just out with the boys." That didn't work.

"What if *I* went out drinkin' with *my* friends 'till all hours of the night?" she sobbed, "and I didn't tell you where I was? And I came home drunk? How would you feel then?"

"Well, Honey, that would be all right with me. Why don't you?" I said weakly. I'd tried my best to reason with her, but that hadn't work at all. I realized then, that when she'd said, 'We need to talk', it meant something quite different than, we should actually talk.

I slept on the old, lumpy sofa that night but the dream came back. I woke up with Fanny standing over me with a fillet knife. I couldn't move my arms or my legs. She was happily singing "The catching was fun but the canning is sweeter. It's so nice to know you've been put up and preserved for the winter of my life." Then the knife came down and I awoke in a cold sweat. I decided that I'd better go and have a talk with Slim.

"You're a damn fool, Schoolteacher," Slim scolded.

"What am I going to do, Slim?"

"Can you cook?"

"Well", I replied, "I still have my 'chick meal."

"Chick meal?" What's that?"

"It's the one really good dinner that I've perfected. It's for when I wanted to impress a girl with my domestic charms. I've used it on a number of occasions back when I was single. It works. It's a whole salmon filled with cream cheese, spinach and lemon wedges then baked to perfection. The chicks dig it." I said proudly.

"Well, it might just work. It's the thought that counts, anyway. Get everything prepared, then go down to Tyler's Mercantile and pick up a bottle of good wine. Right now, get yourself on down to the phone and call the florist in Juneau. Have them send out a dozen fresh, yellow, long-stemmed roses. If those aren't in, then have 'em create something special. Tell 'em it's for a make-up dinner with your fiancé and they'll be sympathetic. Have it delivered on the next float plane. Set the table real pretty and light a candle if you've got one. If not, you can borrow one of my kerosene lanterns. You need some ambiance, Boy."

I was beginning to feel like things might work out. Slim was a genius when it came to women. "What do I talk about, Slim? Should I apologize?"

"Hell yes!" he said. "Tell her that you'll never do it again or that you'll ask her permission next time."

"What?" that was not what I'd wanted to hear.

"Oh, you won't have to really ask. You'll just say something like, 'Honey, how you would feel if I went out and had a beer with Fuzzy?' That should give her the control she needs."

"But… What if she says 'No'?"

"In that case, Mister Married Man, you won't go. That's part of the bargain. Anyway you don't want to harp on what got her mad to begin with, so after sufficient groveling, change the subject to something pleasant."

"Like hunting?"

"No, you imbecile, talk about what she'd like to talk about, like where you're going on your honeymoon or what your children will look like. Try to be suave, and remember, this is all about her."

I did everything that Slim had suggested and it came out fabulously. The wine and the glow of the kerosene mingling with the smell of the fresh flowers put Fanny in a marvelous mood and had the effect of reminding me of why I had considered getting married in the first place. After snuggling on the sofa and talking about our honeymoon, and what our children might look like, we went upstairs and had a wonderful time. Things were back to normal thanks to good old Slim.

During the month leading up to my wedding Slim taught me a wealth of knowledge about women. Over coffee in the pioneers Hall, he pointed to a table of old ladies and had me watch the way they talked to each other. They sat face to face, looking into one another's' eyes as they chatted. Sometimes they actually touched one another on the hand or patted an arm. This, Slim said, was to emphasize that they understood one another, or had something called *empathy* for each other.

Another time we met in the tavern. (I had asked Fanny how she would feel if I went and had a drink with Slim and she was fine with it.) He showed me that men, in stark contrast, prefer to sit on barstools and talk out the sides of their mouths, or look straight ahead and talk to the reflections of their chums in the big mirror behind the bar. They kept their hands in plain sight as a way of showing the other men that they were unarmed. They never touched. (Unless you counted Shorty, who got drunk and put a young logger in a headlock before the kid could break away.)

Slim came to our wedding and gave me this last bit of advice. "Men and women are completely different," he explained. "Men see the big picture in life, while women focus on the minute details. That makes for the great achievements that they can produce when they work together," he told me, "and that is what makes a good union so special. Good luck, Schoolteacher, and may your union always be blessed."

That was the last time I ever saw Slim. He had a heart attack while Fanny and I were in Hawaii on our honeymoon.

Fuzzy got the number to our hotel from the district office over in Angoon. "Hey Schoolteacher," he said on the phone and it sounded like he was right next door. "Sorry to interrupt you guys on your honeymoon, but I thought you should know... Slim passed this morning. Heart attack. We Medevaced him to Juneau but there was nothin' they could do. I know you were his friend..."

I felt my throat constrict and tears welled up in my eyes. I realized that Slim had been a big influence in my life, and I felt sorry that I'd never told him what a great guy I thought he was.

"Just one more thing," Fuzzy stammered, "One of the Coasties on the Medevac helicopter told me that when they went to try to revive him… well, they made a discovery."

"And what was that?" I asked.

"They said that our friend, Slim… Well, he was a woman."

"That figures," I said. Then I set the phone back on the receiver and I cried like a little girl.

Advice

Young fathers to be
You should heed my advice
To throw out the liquor
And give up the dice.
Just do as I say,
But not as I do!
So your blessing be many
And your troubles be few.

THE MURDER OF COLONEL SANDERS

A man should never blame his misfortunes on the actions of his ancestors, and I don't intend to now, although certain oversights by my parents did contribute to the catastrophe of which I here relate. It was precisely these omissions in my upbringing that led me to assume that I could become a successful, if not affluent, chicken rancher in the rainy and sunless climes of southeast Alaska.

The misfortune must also be at least partly a consequence of Homeric fate; a retribution for human pridefullness doled out by some mischievous gods, pagan I assume, because it all began on the Saturday between Good Friday and Easter Sunday and my own God, having been well praised and hallaluiaed, would not have partaken in such a despicable act.

My tale begins without regard to the aforementioned neglects by my own dear mother who, raised on an Oklahoma depression-era farm, strove to isolate me from the hard life of a farmer and in so doing left me without a sufficient background to make intelligent decisions concerning breed or husbandry of domesticated poultry.

So in that incapacitated consciousness I headed off to the hardware store that fateful Saturday, as was my custom. On that particular morning I was accompanied by two of my children, aged three and four, and although I am not the low type of a man to blame his actions on the ascendancy of his children, you will soon understand that their influence did indeed lead to the painful conclusion of this sad enterprise.

Talbot's Hardware is the epitome of a small town hardware store, the type of crowded and confused place that draws me in and delights my senses. They have nuts and bolts, saws, hammers, plungers, paint, and everything a man needs. Except that day... there was something new.

Shining beneath a bare bulb, a cardboard box emitted a soft cacophony on the specific frequency dedicated to the ears of the small and innocent. My own children being thusly configured had no free will to divert their attention. They cooed and awed at the precious contents and bade me bring them home with us. I must admit the creatures in the box were in some small measure soothing to look upon and seemed to harbor a soft intelligence. As I eyed them I lost a portion of my own good sense.

I should relate an episode from years earlier when a professional hypnotist came to our town and, for the purpose of entertainment, called upon the town's respected leaders to appear on stage. Through mystic power of suggestion the stranger caused them to imitate dumb animals. They grazed about the stage, stopping to smell one another's rear ends, and brayed like asses whenever he managed to include in dialog the unobtrusive word "bridge." (Many of us in Ketchikan wonder how long the spell will linger).

I believe a similar type spell was cast upon me for within moments, which are lost to my recollection now, I found myself strapping the children into their car seats and separating them with the mysterious cardboard box, complete with its delicate contents. I returned to the store and emerged with one hundred pounds of a Soylent Green type of mixture which poultry men refer to as "mash".

During my drive home I became aware of an uneasy feeling. I could not precisely identify the source of my dread but the discomfort gave association to the day I'd purchased our home before my wife had seen it. I quickly dismissed any possibility of ill feelings from my wife. She was home with the baby and would surely welcome the companionship of our new acquisitions. These chicks would be a great and practical diversion for her nurturing and nesting feminine propensities.

I soon dismissed my concerns and set about dreaming of my new enterprise. I determined I would need to build a chicken stable. I'd divert the creek through the garden creating a miniature valley complete with stock ponds. Tatsuda's Grocery would take all the extra eggs. I calculated the adjusted gross productivity; six chickens times two eggs a day, times seven days a week, times fifty-two weeks a year. The possibilities were staggering. I'd become an egg magnate!

My wife, Fanny, was less than enthusiastic about the birds. Yes, they were cute; no, I couldn't keep them. I, however, used my masculine prowess effectively, donned the hat of statesman and with eloquent verbiage conscripted my children to the cause. They were fascinated by the political advantages of block voting in a democratic society. After a landslide victory I assured Fanny the chicks would likely die before the week was out. I spent the remainder of the afternoon reassuring the kids that the birds would not die within the week.

So began 'The Good Year'. On quiet summer evenings, at the behest of Fanny, I'd take my guitar into the pasture to pluck and sing my 'good song' until the doggies were lulled fast asleep. Among glistening red feathers brightened to an iridescent hue by the setting sun the proud livestock man serenaded his herd.

I spared no expense creating a comfortable environment for my charges. I built a stable and corral. I purchased bales of straw to line their nests and ran electricity to the stable to control how much light they received and keep the chill off their delicate bones.

One of the chicks grew into a proud bull. He sported a fancy comb and menacing spurs. I alone was granted his respect and was seldom pursued beyond the gates of his domain. The children loved the hens. They were named after saints and often I'd go into the yard to find Agnes and Joan of Arc dressed in baby clothes and bonnets.

I tried to teach them to fly, and with some success I am proud to report. I found their greatest obstacle was the takeoff but with me supplying the initial thrust they achieved nearly twenty yards before gravity pressed them into the beach.

Then came the day I'd prayed for. The day of the egg! We joined as a family while Fanny cooked, then divided it into five equal shares. Each of us, in turn, established it as the most marvelous egg ever eaten. My children were now farm children and given that advantage could compete in the modern world with the self-confidence of our agrarian forefathers. Those were the good times and as winter approached I dreamed of increasing the size of my holdings and of the eggs I'd sell to pay for my children's postsecondary education.

Colonel Sanders, as the bull came to be called, had been named after that wizened and whitened promoter of poultry. But unlike the smiling southern gentleman, my bird grew increasingly dangerous and domineering. The children began to fear him and Fanny likened him to his terrible ancestors, the Veloceraptors. The evil bird assumed many primordial characteristics of his cruel and carnivorous ancestors. His beady, diabolic eyes seemed always to search for opportunity to attack. No doubt the link between modern aviary and the terrible beasts of the Jurassic era is more kindred than the Darwinians can yet validify.

To make matters worse, the demonic bird developed an inaccurate crowing chronometer caused, regrettably, by my electric light. He crowed every morning at 2:45a.m., which had the effect of provoking the neighbors to treat me with hostility.

As winter wore on the neighbors became increasingly mean and irreverent to my being a livestock owner. Each morning at 2:45 I would get a phone call during which the caller insinuated awful and untrue things about me and my chickens, often using profanity to make some remote point about sleeplessness.

Then my loving wife of many years turned against me. I'd have to cut the bull from my herd as the ultimatums were becoming serious and profound. One morning, after a particularly nasty communiqué, I committed. Colonel Sanders must die!

And so it was that early on the morning of December 1 I solemnly loaded my pellet pistol, all along reciting "Hail Mary" and asking God's forgiveness for what I was about to do.

I entered the kitchen with the heavy pistol cradled in my palm, but hid it quickly in my sportcoat pocket when I noticed my wife and children sitting up folding laundry.

"You goin' to do it," she reaffirmed.

I nodded in reply and stepped outside. I stood beside the door trembling but resolute in the successful completion of my horrid assignment. I went to the storage room and procured a stoat box to serve as a coffin. I then proceeded to the corral.

What sad emotions rose in my gorge as I saw my beloved Colonel. So calm, he seemed, that I had no doubt he possessed a precognition as to the solemnity of the occasion. He looked innocent and dignified, displaying not a hint of aggression toward me, which had the effect of softening my resolve.

When I called to him he responded immediately and I simply reached down and picked him up. I began a discourse of his many tribulations but he grew nervous and flapped wildly until I hypnotized him with the great Weisnewski Chicken Mesmerizing Feat.

I knelt on the cold ground and made the sign of the cross. For all the world, I felt like Abraham about to plunge a knife into Isaac and wished for a ram to appear in a thorny bush and for God to stay my hand. But God was not to show himself yet that morning and so, holding Colonel Sanders with one hand, I held the pistol hard against the back of his head and fired the loathsome weapon.

The colonel quivered beneath my hand and was still. I lifted his soft, warm body and reverently laid him to rest him in his coffin. I placed the box in the garbage can and replaced the lid. Once more I prayed for the soul of my chicken, "God take this creature to Chicken Heaven," I pleaded. "He was a good chicken, Lord. Amen."

I returned to the house and was surprised to see all three children sitting in a circle watching their dear mother fold laundry. "Kids, Colonel Sanders has gone missing. I'm sorry."

Fanny and I glanced at one another knowingly. His death shouldn't be a lingering sadness for the children but I was astonished that the children were not at all distraught by his absence. They had become true farm children and for them life and death had become the natural cycle in the world. I said my good-byes and headed for work.

Hurrying by the garbage I was surprised to find the lid ajar. Upon closer inspection I found the coffin empty.

In a panic I searched the area. As I worked my way around the house I found him. He would not come to my call for I had lost his trust. I chased him until I was out of breath then picked up a rock and chucked it at him. These words filled my mind, "Let he who is without sin cast the first stone." But sin or no sin the stone found its mark and I "whooped" in triumph as the bird tumbled onto the beach. Attempting to escape he crawled into a hole, but the measure of my arm was longer than the depth of the hole, and so I had him.

I held him down on the gravelly beach and with a large stone attempted to crush his head. Again and again I hammered. Each time, he flopped his head at the final instant avoiding the fatal blow. This rhythm went on for several measures until I inserted a quarter rest and achieved synchronization. The stone connected with the discordant tone of shattering bone.

I slumped on the beach with head in hands. I'd murdered Colonel Sanders. Taking a deep breath I grabbed him by a leg and scurried around the back of the house. In my frenzied state I clumsily slipped on the muddy trail and let go of the bird to catch myself. Death must have lost his mighty grip for upon contact with the ground the misshapen bird bolted into the salmonberry-snarled undergrowth and disappeared.

"Shoot!" I shouted. I looked down at my watch realizing I'd soon be late for work.

I entered the house a defeated man. "Kids, Colonel Sanders is really sick. His head looks deformed. He has a disease so keep away from him."

"What!!" Fanny scolded.

"Is Colonel Sanders going to die, Daddy?"

"Yes kids, he is. But I've got to get to work." I returned Fanny's glare. "I'll take care of the Colonel when I get home." And I left…again.

Approaching my car I spied him behind the rear tire. My first thought was to run him over but knew he would dart at the sound of the engine. Like a jungle cat I crept around the car. He was up in an instant tearing toward the beach. I sprinted close behind feeling the thrill of the chase. My every muscle reacted, strong and determined. The blood of ancestral predators pumped through my veins. My demeanor changed. My hands assumed the attitude of claws. I prepared for the final lunge to bring down my prey, to rip him to shreds. But instead …I witnessed a miracle.

Colonel Sanders flew! I felt the thrill of exaltation as I watched my flying lessons come to fruitful conclusion. He arched over the ocean gracefully (except for the odd angle at which his head bobbed beneath a wing) and landed back on the beach in full stride. He headed to the embankment and dove into the very same hole in which he had sought sanctuary before.

I felt glorious in my victory. I reached into the hole, grabbed him by the neck, and gave a great whip-like jerk. His head came off in my fist and his body tumbled down the beach. I gazed into the eye and as life ebbed away, so too did the hypnotic spell which had held me in the service of chickens these past many months.

I quickly grabbed up his lifeless form and trotted for the garbage cans. Without ceremony I stuffed him into the box and placed a large stone upon the top. I crammed it into the garbage can, slammed down the lid and hoisted a cinder block onto the whole kit and caboodle.

I flung open the door. "Colonel Sanders is dead!" I hollered. Quickly regaining my composure I added, "He died in my arms, children. He's in heaven now."

"Are you certain?" queried my wife.

"Dead certain."

My chicken ranching days are over. I gave my herd to the janitor at work. Sadly, I must report that they were killed one night by a prowling dog.

Draw what conclusions you must as to my behavior on that fateful day. I must live with the terrible guilt and make restitution at the feet of Saint Peter on the day of my reckoning. I have kept in my heart some pleasant memories of those happy months and will miss singing to my herd on the rain soaked coast of southeast Alaska. And I'm given great comfort in knowing that, if the wind is right, and with the help of a good teacher, even an old bull can feel the wind beneath his wings and fly over the ocean and into the cradling arms of God.

On Connell Lake

Still the harsh cusp between winter and spring
 was looming down the Ides of March.
Beware the sadness of this anticipatory season,
still infertile and nervously waiting in the stark cold.

We need to change our positions; to get up and out and enter in, to join the absolute and take our part. We must inhale
the icy breath
and feel the unity of natural things,
To exhale the warm camaraderie
of shared experience.

I stumble behind the timid white dog.
My two grown children are up ahead
sharing a laugh together.
I struggle to catch up.

The cedar woods are quiet.
The sky is dark
and spits the odd snow-sleet
onto dirty drifts beneath the still sleeping giants.
We find a frozen trail of broken crusts,
sharp and unbalanced
to twist and turn my worn knees.

The black and white stream whispers.
Everyone is whispering.

We feel the kite of Spring-Hope fly
with the paired bald eagles.
Swooping through the aisle of trees
above the dancing stream,
shrugging off the taunting ravens.

Here the puny alders lay siege
to reclaim the old pipeline road.
We step gently through the tangled web,
camouflaged in grey-black wool
to blend into the still life.

A painting of three people
separated in a thicket of leafless trees.
The one who looks like you
is twenty feet behind the others.
They stand motionless in the alder grove.
But then the white dog moves.

We climb up from the river to the outfall of the dam. The
children walk above me
on the old wooden pipeline.

I climb the shaky steel ladder
to calm the frightened dog
who will not step on the rusting orange grates,
while the rushing water and mysterious black eddies are
swirling below.

The free waters roar

with unrestrained delight
and spew out industriously
to join the river below
in a steaming, icy froth.

A huge tree trunk, precariously wedged,
guards the concrete dam.
An uncomfortable balance
high above the white reservoir.

A pair of footprints, undefined and windswept,
head away from shore, far out onto the frozen lake until they
disappear into the whiteness.
They do not return.

The whole frozen surface, acres and acres,
have dropped with the outflow at the dam
and huge, heavy slabs of ice
slope steeply downward
and break onto the white plains below.

 We sit on our butts
 and slide down the long slippery slabs,
 laughing.
The lake ice groans and threatens.
We are alone.

We spread out to distribute our weight
 and send the dog ahead.
 Hoping she's retained some malamute memory,

our sacrificial canary
 in a white crystal mine.

We walk tenderly,
keeping our weight above us,
and note every crack and fissure
that interrupts the smoothness of the plate.
We point to low spots
 and freeze with each changing sound
as we step from soft snow to crunchy ice.

Here and there, ancient trees,
once buried in the flood,
 poke their dead heads above the winter-white lake. And
cradle their marbled ice-children
 in twisted branches, like towering nannies
 protecting their babes.
While ringed fangs of open water
tear at their cotton aprons.

The groaning icemen, in deep baritone,
piously chant a celibate warning
as frigid waters drift beneath their long, white robes.
The whole massive sheet shivers and strains.
So do we.

We make our way toward the shore, one at a time,
 to climb along a fissure between two hulking slabs until we
are above the lake and on a rugged shore clogged with silver
driftwood.

A psychotic landscape of imbalanced,
crisscrossing logs
that teeter and fall.
And push us into a maze of traps,
Surrounded by devil's club and precipice.
we retreat back onto the dangerous ice.

There is no chatter on this nervous crossing,
A silent and deliberate shuffle.
In recent tracks that held us once,
 (We hope again),
Finally, one by one,
we scurry up the slick-slope
and breathe deeply in relief…
Our smiling has a cause.

On the road we break a giant icicle
from the rocky cliff
and try to ride it like a sled.
It keeps getting stuck in the ruts
so we shove it over the edge.
 It crashes down the cliff and into the river below.

We find our car and drive home in quiet reflection. The
white dog is sick and dry-heaving in the back. (She's frightened crazy of riding in the car.)

In the west, a crimson stain
spills up into the darkening canvas.

Pride an' Prejudice

My friend, Wazoo, is what most folks would call a *Specialist*; someone who learns more and more about less and less until he knows everything about almost nothing at all. I, on the other hand, consider myself a *Generalist*; one who learns less and less about more and more until I know just a little, teeny bit about everything. Together we make a fine pair.

We have been friends since we were just little kids and so I can say for certain that Wazoo considers himself to be the smartest man he's ever met. He has a PhD. in an obscure area of science and he can talk your ear off about it without ever explaining what it actually is. Of all my friends to poke fun at, Wazoo is just plain the funnest.

A little indicator of the kind of shenanigans I like to pull to get Wazoo's goat might be exemplified by the time we went to the drive-in movies in his old 1958 Caddy. While we were watching the movie I reached down and found a little wire hanging down by the passenger door. When I touched the wire to the metal on the door, voila, the dome light came on!

"Wazoo, shut off your stupid dome light so we can watch the movie!" I said.

The great Wazoo tried every knob in that big car but couldn't seem to make it go out. Finally, I suggested that he pick his feet up off the floorboards, and what do you know? The light went out. A few minutes later that pesky light came on again.

"Wazoo! What are you doing? Turn off that stupid light!" Again, he frantically exhausted every plausible solution until I suggested that he take his hands off the steering wheel. And low and behold...

Well, I guess you can see where this is leading. By the end of the movie I had WZ curled up in a little ball in the backseat. I suppose that I became a little carried away with my powers because the next time that dome light came on, he jumped out of the car, went to the trunk and grabbed a little ball peen hammer, and before I could say another word he smashed the dome light to smithereens. He was so proud of himself for fixing the light that I decided never to tell him about the loose wire.

Wazoo is one heck of a fly-fisherman and he takes his fishing, like he takes himself, *very* seriously. He looks like the poster child for a fly-fishing catalog: the fly-encrusted hat, the cute vest, and the chest-highs. And as for really expensive gear, you name it, and he's got it dangling somewhere. Of course he ties his own flies and gives them original names like The Grand Wazoo. That would be his special fly. It's really just a simple Deer-Hair Yellow but he makes it sound like it's the hardest fly to tie in the whole wide world and he makes fun of the way I tie it. Here's how: Wrap the shank of a hook with yellow tape, take a clump of deer hair and strap it on somehow just behind the eye. TaDaa! A Grand Wazoo. As much as I like to make fun of it, that fly really is a very good fly for the Yellowstone River, especially when the water is clear.

One day WZ asked me to go fishin' with him. We were going to float the Yellowstone River from Carter's Bridge down to Livingston, Montana. It was one of our favorite floats but that particular day the wind was beginning to blow, and as the saying goes, "The wind doesn't *blow* in Livingston, it *sucks*!" There are places in the river that are wide and slow, so that if it really blows, you ain't goin' anywhere.

Fly-fishing in that kind of wind is unproductive. I mentioned this to Wazoo and said that I was bringing my spinning rod. Just the words *Spinning Rod*, had a most adverse affect on WZ. He would spit and drool and get all uppity. There is no greater insult to a fly-fisherman that to suggest spinning gear (Except for suggesting the use of worms).

"Maybe I should dig you some worms, WZ, just in case the Grand Wazoo fails you in the wind."

Choke...Gasp...Puke...

We put in at Carter's bridge and sure enough the wind came up. WZ and I were sitting back to back. He was manning the oars because, like I said, it was too windy for fly fishing and he wouldn't lower himself to use spinning gear.

The other trouble was that there had been a storm down in the park and the river was running a bit muddy. Not terribly bad, but enough so that the big German Browns were feeding by scent, if at all, and the only thing I was catching were the worthless, bony whitefish with their disgusting rubbery lips. 'Whitefish are good smoked' as the saying goes, 'but they're hard to keep lit.' Anyway, I was catching just a load of whitefish on a Mepp's #3 gold with the red cut off and I could hardly keep 'em off my hook. Then I had a great idea...

"WZ," I said, "There are so many whitefish in this stretch! Every cast I'm having two or three fish following the one I catch right up to the raft."

"Well," he replied haughtily, "If you were using a fly, you wouldn't be having these problems."

"You're right, but I think that the way these fish are behaving today, maybe a fella could catch two fish on the same hook. That would be a sporty thing to accomplish. Don't you think?"

I was baiting more than the fish now. Wazoo was all about *sporting*. If he was going on a hike it had to be at least twenty miles. If he went on a hunt; bow and arrows. To fish; flies only. To golf; NO carts, ever. He was *all* about Sporting.

"You'll never catch two fish on one hook, even if you use a treble hook." He spat.

I didn't even turn around, but I distinctly heard him scowl when said "treble hook". Little did he know that I had three, very large, very fresh and kicking whitefish in the bottom of the raft tucked out of sight at my feet. And even as he spoke, I was attaching them one by one until all three were secured to the aforementioned treble hook. When WZ was busy fighting the wind as we came around the next bend, I lowered my mighty prize into the drink.

I gave my catch a great deal of slack and kept just the slightest tension on the line to keep them in a gentle tow. And then I waited. I was at the very limit of my patience when I finally offered to row the raft for a while. I would have to hope that the fish stayed caught for a little while longer or Wazoo might become suspicious.

We changed positions and I spotted an osprey on the bank. Diverting his attention to the bird, I reached back and set my bail to free spool.

"DOG-ON-IT!" I hollered as we approached the next bend of the river. "WZ, my bale is free-spooling. Grab my rod and see if you can save the lure." Then I put my back into the oars and acted as if I had nothing to think about but the wind and the water.

Wazoo, on the other hand, soon became very excited. "I've got something on here! It's not fightin' very hard, but it sure is heavy. This thing's huge. Get out the net. This one's a lunker!"

"It's probably just a whitefish, but don't horse it," I cautioned as I handed him the net. "Here, net it yourself or we'll get blown back upstream." And once again, I put my back into the oars."

"Holy..., WAZOO!" he screamed (hence the nickname), "I caught three whitefish on the same spinner! There's one fish on each of the three hooks!"

"No way!" I replied feigning disbelief. "That's amazing! No, that's *sporting*! Way to go DoubleYouZee!" I exclaimed while congratulating him whole-heartedly with a manly back-slap.

Since that memorable trip Wazoo and I have shared many more fishing adventures. Oftentimes, he invites one of his yuppity-uppity, fly-fishing purist friends. Invariably, the topic will move to the Zen and sportiness of fly-fishing.

And whenever Wazoo begins to expound on the unworthiness of other types of gear, I will slyly suggest, "Hey WZ, tell us about the time you caught the three whitefish on a single treble hook."

And guess what fellas? Rock beats scissors, scissors beats paper, and pride beats prejudice... every time.

Lost

The farther along
I needed to go,
The further behind
 I got.
So pausing to let
The world catch up,
 I rediscovered
Who I was,
And who
I was
Not.

Cannibals!

I don't know, even now, as I sit here much later in my life meditating about how I came to be the man that I have come to be, if I ever truly believed that those cruel Texas oilmen were actually cannibals who ate small boys. They were camped at the outcropping near the Twisted Cedar just below our hunting camp high up on The Gore Pass in the fall of 1965. As I was a small boy at the time, I probably had more at stake in the rumors than I do now; and being somewhat less worldly than I am today, some fifty years later, I can conclude that whether or not the rumors of cannibals were actually true, I certainly had my own inklings, and I can recall that my nightmares were real enough.

The Texans started out as an extremely friendly bunch. Sporting all the best in hunting gear including, my father once confided, the most excellent single-malt scotch whiskey. "But avoid their camp like the plague, Son," he'd told me, "for they have sinnin' going on there that'll permanently close the pearly gates to him who partakes. And if you show up with tarnish on your soul such as those men are sportin', Saint Peter would sooner toss the keys the Keys to Heaven into a beaver pond, than to allow such a sinner to pass through."

The first few weekends of huntin' season it seemed like all the men in our camp were bound to become the best of chums with those Texas men. My dad and our partners would go down to the Texas Camp and laugh and hoot until all hours of the night. Me and the other boys would curl up in our sacks after a hard day of hunting' and dream of the next big buck or bull elk we'd see out on the trail.

Long about midnight our men would return to camp trying to be quiet, but waking us up every time with their slurred chuckles and guffaws.

A few hours later, we boys would get stuck doing' all of the morning chore including making coffee and breakfast. The men would rub their eyes and cough a lot. On those mornings, after they'd been to the Texas Camp, they didn't seem to be as excited about hunting as we boys were.

One night, I awoke suddenly and could have sworn that I heard female voices echoing off the canyon walls. Another time, after the men had been to Texas Camp, they slept in and told all of us boys to go out hunting by ourselves. "Just stay on The Crested Knoll," they'd warned, "and keep away from The Twisted Cedar." The Knoll was the mountaintop where we'd placed our hunting camp for those many years. The Twisted Cedar, at the bottom of the Steep Grade, was where the Texas Camp was.

There were four boys in camp that weekend. Two were teenagers and another was about my age and we were all just smiling as big as all get out. We were finally considered regular men and could go off hunting with our fathers rifles.

I was only ten years old at the time and my Dad said I would have to take the 22 caliber rifle and be content just to hunt grouse and squirrels. But I was in heaven, a boy and his gun alone in the woods, this was the life, and I was appreciating every second of it.

As a young boy I could creep up on just about any critter. I was so quiet and small that everything else in the woods thought I was harmless. But I could shoot that 22. Within a few hours I had shot seven squirrels.

Now, killing animals is a strange thing. The first thing I always felt was a pride at being such a good shot. But then, as I retrieved the little critters, another emotion would catch up with me. Sorrow.

When I looked into the eye of a squirrel as it was dying I wanted to cry. I was never a sissy-boy, but I guess taking the life of another living thing always has consequences. For me it was a feeling of guilt. I'd read in one of my many books about camping and hunting that the Indians used to thank the animal for giving itself to them after they had killed it. I figured this to be a good practice and have done it ever since.

"Thank you, squirrel, for giving yourself to me. I will eat you and you will help me grow into a big, strong man." I'd said.

I had a wonderful day doing boy things; mainly just climbing on stuff like rocks and trees, and playing at being Daniel Boone. I was the Fess Parker of my own imagination.

I found a creek and slunk along an old game trail before coming back to the Jeep trail. Skirting back towards camp I enjoyed poking at a porcupine that wasn't smart enough to keep out of my way. That's about the time I came upon the Dozer.

To a boy there's no better playground than a big, yellow Bull Dozer. I set down the squirrels and climbed all over that big dozer. Out here on the mountain it seemed odd and out of place. It was hidden from the Jeep Road that came down off the Crested Knoll. That was the only road into the hunting grounds. It wound along the Sagebrush Ridge, down to the Beaver Ponds and back into the Black Timber Country where we hunted for elk.

Eventually, I grew bored with the dozer. There were no keys to try and start it with, and the entire world lay before me to explore.

When I arrived back at camp late that afternoon I showed my dad the squirrels. His response was less than impressed. I had imagined that he would be proud and brag me up to the other men.

Instead he hollered over to Duane who was busy barbequing something that smelled fantastic. "Hold off on cookin' up a steak for my boy, Duane. He's gone and hunted up his own dinner."

Then he turned to me and told me to quick get those squirrels skinned and cooled, and to fetch some sticks on which to skewer them for roasting. "Seven grey mountain squirrels seems like a big meal for a boy your size, but I suppose that you've worked up quite an appetite today. Bon Appetite, Sonny"

All the men and boys gathered around our big fire pit and instructed me as to the best way to grill squirrel. It didn't take me too long to figure out that there is NO best way to grill squirrel. The meat was grey and stringy and either burnt to a crisp or still soft and chewy. After two or three, I was feeling a little green. When the men were distracted with their own dinners, I fiddled with adjusting the sticks until, thankfully, they caught fire and the little meat kabobs met their fate in the silvery ash.

I was expecting criticism for wasting meat but just then one of the Texans burst into camp like a wildman.

"Are all of you fella's alright up here? Is anyone hurt?" he asked. The big man was genuinely worried that someone in our party had been hurt.

The men of camp all seemed to stand up straighter, to grow a little taller, the way men do when action is required. They all looked around at each of us boys. We all stood with open hands and shrugged to show that we were alright.

"We're all fine here, Mister. Why? What's going on?" Duane spoke for all the men.

"Oh, I guess it's nothin' much," said the Texan acting a bit sly, "We just found blood on some of our equipment and thought maybe one of your boys had hurt himself. It's good to see that all of you boys are alright. I guess I'll just be on my way then. So long." And the man scurried back out of our camp as fast as he had come in.

When the man had gone, Duane called a camp meeting. We gathered around the fire pit. Everyone was wondering what the man had been asking about. I was still feeling a bit sickly from my cookin' when Dad asked me show my hands.

"I'm fine, Dad, really. No blood on me 'ceptin' fer a little squirrel blood."

"Were you messin' around on any of those Texan's rigs?" Duane asked.

"No Sir," was my honest reply, "I was just climbing around on an old bulldozer that I found down in the draw."

"A bulldozer? Down in the draw? Why would there be a dozer up here?"

"Well," said Duane, "I heard down in town that a group of fellas bought the Bar-S. That's the ranch that runs along the river from State Bridge all the way up to the Sagebrush Ridge. They were planning on making a game preserve, really a private hunting ranch. If they could build their own road up from the ranch, then pull the culvert out of the draw, it would close off the access to this whole area to everyone except the ranch clients."

"But this is BLM land! They can't close this road. That would close our hunting area!" All the men were angry now and we boys were getting' excited too. They asked me to lead them to where I'd found the dozer. I led the way as we all trudged through the woods down to the draw.

When we got there, the men all commented on the blood that was all over the steps on the dozer's cab. "Oh," I said, "that's just a little squirrels blood!" Everyone got a big chuckle out of that. It seemed that I'd become a hero of sorts for finding the dozer.

The men decided to head on into town the next morning and take their concerns to the authorities.

That was the end of any cordial relationships between us and the Texas men. In fact, things got down-right nasty and I guess that's when I first found out that they might be cannibals.

Men say a lot of mean things about each other. Even when they're good friends, they do a lot of teasing that, to an outsider, could sound just plain mean. But that kind of ribbing stands aside to the type of language men will use when they are *really* angry. Say, at a group of fellas who tried in an underhanded way to close off their legal access to a

hunting ground that they have been using for gen-
erations. That kind of mean talk is the kind where
women blush and children hold their ears closed.

A few days after the dozer incident a BLM
man in pale green Ford Bronco bucked his way up
to The Crested Knoll and talked to our men. Then
he went down and had a look at the dozer before
heading over to the Texas camp.

A few hours later we could hear that dozer
start up and we all went out on the ledge to watch
as it as an angry Texan in a big grey hat walked it
back down the ravine toward State Bridge and the
Bar-S.

The Texas camp had grown much smaller by
November and the men who had stayed seemed of
a harder type. There were no more sounds of wom-
en in the night, no more forays for the good scotch
by our men, and no more friendly salutes.

In fact, you could feel the nervous tension
whenever we had to drive by their camp. Coming
up The Steep Grade before the Knoll we had to go
right by them. Sometimes the men made aggressive
gestures to one another.

One time, when I was in the back of the
Wagoneer and we had passed their camp, the
meanest of 'em stepped out behind the Jeep and

stared hard right into my eyes. Then he made a sign like he was cutting his throat with his finger. But he was staring straight at me while he was doing it.

"You stay away from those Texas men," my father warned me. "They would chew you up and spit you out as soon as look at you!"

Later in the season, during elk, one of the other boys had a run in with that mean one. He was on the same drive as I was. We boys were spread out and walking up a big draw. The men were stationed on points along both sides of the draw. The oldest of the men had stations of honor near the meadow at the end of the drive.

That boy had wandered too high up the hillside to the north and came face to face with the mean man, the ugly one, who always wore a big, grey cowboy hat.

The boy later said that he heard a noise and turned, and then he saw the Texan up on a rocky point. He had his rifle pointed right at the boy and his finger on the trigger! That boy high tailed it at a full run. And when he did, the whole hillside came alive. Bucks, and does, and bulls, and cows all runnin' like wild up the draw. And then the shootin' started. It sounded like World War Three! When it was all done our tags were filled and that boy, the one who'd been spooked so bad, he was the hero of our camp!

The Texans grew even madder.

We celebrated all night, and they must have heard, but the best part was the next morning. They drove by our camp about an hour before first light. We were all awake but in no hurry on account of we had filled all of our tags, so it was sit and drink your coffee and look smug time.

Those Texas men lit up their spotlights and shone 'em in our camp to see a great string of bull elk and timber bucks hanging neatly in a row. To a hunter, it was a sight to behold.

The next week at school droned on and on. Having to go to school during huntin' season was torture for a boy. Friday evening finally came and I sat out in the Wagoneer waiting for my dad to get home from work. By the time we left the house it had started to snow hard. The closer we got to State Bridge, the worse the weather became. At the bottom of The Gore, the highway patrol had set up a roadblock.

"Where are you folks headed tonight?" the patrolman asked my father. He shined his flashlight in at me.

"We're headed up The Gore to our hunting camp. How's the road from here?"

"It's open if you've got chains. The weather is expected to let up before morning. Where is your camp?"

We're near the top, to the south, up Crested Knob country."

"Up in the Black Timber?"

"No, not that high."

"The reason I ask is because we've got a search team up there looking for a lost hunter. Two actually, a man and his boy."

"Texans?"

"No, these were from Michigan."

"Oh yea, I know that group. They were tent camping up near the Beaver Ponds."

That's them. Keep a lookout for 'em and contact us if you come across them.

"Will do. G'night officer."

We pulled over to chain up and lock in the hubs for our four wheel drive. The snow had stopped falling and the clouds were braking up enough to show a big full moon intermittently.

We slid, and bounced, and jumped along the Jeep Trail until we came to the bottom of the Steep Grade.

As we were coming up to the Steep Grade the moon poked out again and lit up the Crested Knoll. Now, normally I would get a warm feeling when we got to that point of the Trail. When I could see that ancient silver tree we all called Twisted Cedar, then I knew we were almost back to camp. But that night something was terribly wrong.

On the rocky ridge just below our camp we could see the fires from the Texas Camp reflecting off the trees. It was an eerie sight. In the flickering flames, the shadows of men seemed to be dancing off the rock ledge. We couldn't see the men themselves just those haunting ghost-like shadows. When we got up even with their camp, my father and I came upon the most horrifying sight that a mortal man can bear to see; one that has burned its way into my brain for all these many years.

There, in the cold moonlight was the figure of a man hanging from the old Twisted Cedar at the outcropping by the Texas Camp. He had been stripped of all his skin and his head was gone. His arms were spread, and his wrists were tied to a branch so that his feet dangled but a few inches above the snowy ground.

"Oh my God! What have they done?" screamed my father.

"They have found and killed the lost hunters!" I surmised. "And they're cookin' and eatin' his boy!"

Dad hit the gas and we flew up the Steep Grade faster than I ever thought it could be done. We hit it bumps so hard that I flew up out of my seat and cracked my head on the roof of the cab.

When we got to our camp, Dad brought the Wagoneer to a sliding stop and called out for all the men to gather at the fire pit. He told the men about the lost hunters and about the hanging man. The men all grew taller and Duane suggested that they take up their rifles.

They sent us boys into the big tent with instructions not to come out until they'd returned. Off they went to the Twisted Tree, The Texas Camp, and to probable doom.

We boys sat huddled together in The Big Tent and scared each other worse by forecasting outcomes of a failed expedition. I was holding my .22 and had the clip of bullets ready if it should be needed.

When the men finally returned they were in a strange mood. They were chuckling, and kept elbowing my dad in a lighthearted way.

I stuck my head through the tent flaps, "Well, what the heck happened?" I hollered.

Duane was the first man to come into the fire-light. He pushed back his hat and laughed so hard that I thought he'd gone plumb nuts.

"Bear" he said. "Your daddy 'bout soiled his pants for the sight of a skinned bear!" All the men, including my dad, had a great long laugh then.

Now that I'm an older man, I realize that I wasn't the only one haunted by the thought of cannibals in the Texas Camp. My father would never forget it. Not as long as Duane, and Elmer, and Glen were alive. No Sir, he never would be allowed to forget…

Archipelago

The smooth sea
Swirls metallic,
Calmly tempestuous,
Dangerously pacific.

Skyscape, seascape
Landscapes mingle.
Blended and mixed,
Churning and changing
Shapes and shades
Of gradient greens and greys.
Payne's Grey,
And Davies Grey
A vaporous viridian,
A single burst
of broken-blue.
And wet!

Whipping strands of bull kelp,
Beached, half coiled,
Invite the rambling boy,
Inspire the rawhide dream.
Burnt umber mud
Sucks my brown rubber boots.

Living sprinklers
Toss sea to sky.
Mullusk-gysered sea fountains
Triumphant.
Goosetongue thrives
In tidewater cleft.
Shimmering, slick
Paper-thin seaweed
Glows like neon
Plastic sushi sleeves.

Rumbling, crumbling,
Tumbling gravel,
Shifting shale
Hush my footfall.
The great blue heron fishes here.
So do I.

Devil's club barricades the beach.
Guarding secret island cedar
Lifting fog and sunlight
Breaching, reaching,
Warming, Jesus rays
Beckon and beacon
The acre island

Where I stand
Steaming and sweating,
Alive and alone
Between the two
Mysterious headstones.
Alice Koosnick 1892
John White 1897
The mist absorbs
My whispered prayer,

"Rest here in this restless place…
…In peace."

Lessons From a Ride Home

"Howdy Son, climb on in. How was school today?"

"Fine."

"Did you show everyone the car ya built?"

"Yep, but I painted it blue with orange flames before school this morning."

"Sounds cool. What kind of machines did the other kids bring in?"

"One kid built a car that runs on pancakes."

"Pancakes?"

"Yea, but he hasn't worked the bugs out yet."

"What was the coolest machine?"

"One kid brought in a cow that poops. And it has baby bottle nipples for its *you-know-whats.*"

"Really? Does it push out little candies when you lift up its tail, like one of those moose poop gadgets that they sell in the tourist shops?"

"Nope. Pudding!"

"Pudding! That sounds pretty messy. What kid built that contraption?"

"Gracie."

"Gracie! Well, I guess that figures."

"Slug bug blue. No slug backs."

"OUCH! You know, when I retire from teachin', I'm going to get me one of them slug bugs. A red one. And then I'm gonna drive around all day watchin' kids smack each other on their arms. I'll circle every playground in town, twice a day, just watchin' those kids pound each other an' say, 'Slug bug red, no slug backs.' That'll be my pay-back for all those nasty little boys actin' up in my classroom for twenty-some years. Yes sir, revenge is a dish best served cold! ..."

"WHOO-WEE! Did you let one? Somethin' smells mighty odiferous"

"It wasn't me."

"Well, it wasn't me neither, and seein' how there's just the two of us in this truck, then it had to be you."

"Maybe we drove through a cloud of bad gas. Someone must have been burnin' rotten eggs, and plastic, and dead rats. Open up the winders."

"Won't that just let in more bad gas?"

"Nope, we already picked up the bad gas and now its circilatin' in the car. I'm openin' my wind-er."

"Whew, that's better. I guess you were right, must o' just passed through a bad gas cloud."

"Speakin' of smelly, Dad, whatever you do, don't ever throw a beetle into a bug zapper."

"Yea? What do you mean?"

"Expecially them big ol' Stink Bugs."

"Pretty bad, huh?"

"It's the very most horrible, worst smell on the planet earth!"

"Had experience with that, have ya?"

"Yep, lesson learnt the hard way."

An Informal Disquisition

I am fond of the word
disquisition.
I praise the musical lilt
of each distinct syllable.
The schwa, the soft short i's.
"An informal disquisition,"
It rolls around my mouth
like a sweet Bing cherry,
like a lover's tongue,
an operatic measure.
It means; a treatise,
basically.
Which doesn't do
much for me.
But
"Disquisition"
   Aahh!

The Luck o' the Irish

"And there's a hand, my trusty fiere
And gie's a hand o' thine
And we'll take a right gud-wellie waught
For auld lang syne."
Robert Burns

Our heritage contributes a great deal to our personalities. Our family lineage becomes a part of who we are and provides us with a foundation on which to build our lives. I am relating this as a man who was raised by an Irish-Presbyterian mother and a German-Lutheran father, and who married an English-Bohemian Catholic. Of all of these influences it has been my dear, Irish mother who had the greatest influence in my life.

As stated previously, I was raised as an Irish-American-German Lutheran. And each of these particular traits affected the way in which I ordered my life. From the Germans I acquired a scheduled timetable. I hate to be late for anything. And there is a sense of orderliness in my life, the Germans are a clean and orderly people and so, in most things, am I. From the Lutherans I got a bit of rebelliousness and a whole slew of Christian values. But most of all, from the Lutherans, I received a persistent and obnoxious outspokenness. When I see something that's just plain wrong, I'll tell you about it. And I won't shut up until right's been wronged or the problem's been fixed.

Sometimes, when I have to apologize for my big mouth, I just say, "Jesus, I'm sorry. It's the Lutheran in me talkin'." Most folks will nod understandingly and forgive me.

From the Irish I got my luck, my love of potatoes, and the appreciation of good whiskey and beer. (The love of beer may also be a Germanic contribution, which when coupled with my Irishness can cause me to overindulge on occasion.) I do like my beer, and that's a fact.

My wife and I had a series of debates about religion when we had first begun having children shortly after our wedding. Fanny was pregnant with our first child and the crux of the discussions revolved around which of our respective religions would become the spiritual foundation for our soon to be family. We debated the merits of each of our prospective belief systems and eventually Martin

Luther and I won out. The kids would be raised as good little Lutherans just as I had been.

I can imagine that my parents must have had, sometime after the Second World War, a similar conversation. And although I never researched the arguments applied by each of my parents, I am acutely aware of the outcome. My father's Lutheranism somehow defeated my mother's conglomerate of Protestant, Southern Baptist, Methodist and Presbyterianism. I resolved that my Grandmother, a devout Lutheran, had some influence on the decision, as did my dear Uncle Otto, a Lutheran minister.

As a young Irish-American I celebrated St. Patrick's Day with great passion. It began early on with the wearing of green socks and the pinching of the non-believers. Eventually, it led to walking in parades and to pub crawls which intermingled into surreal and dreamy celebrations dedicated to a great saint who drove the serpents from the Emerald Isle. I remember owning a green and orange baseball cap that said, "Kiss Me, I'm Irish." It had little green lights around the brim that flashed on and off with mesmerizing consistency, and encouraged many a red-haired lass to taste the sweet goods beneath the brim.

It was at these times in my life that my pride of ancestry was at its zenith. I possessed within my heart, and in my mind a powerful and great gift, the certainty of knowing that I was invincible, for I had received on the day of my birth the fabled Luck of the Irish. And I, being strong and able in mind and spirit, would never succumb to the slings and arrows of outrageous fortune.

Because of my certainty in the absolute power of that inherited gift, the gift of manifest protection, and therefore, being well isolated from the pains and hardships which had brought other young men to their knees, I became a fearless and self-confident young man.

When my compatriots and I would leap from the high cliffs into the frigid waters of Blue Mesa Reservoir I would climb even higher and exceed all other jumpers with my unbridled courage. When we rafted down the mighty rivers of the west, I would choose the wildest trajectories and emerge from the froth relatively unscathed.

No dare was too outrageous for my attempt and my friends would often comment while they extolled their congratulatory slaps on my back, "Billy, you were surely born with the Luck o' the Irish."

To which I would respond, "I know it. And a hearty thanks to me dear Irish Mum!"

But nothing lasts forever. Most people will begin to change very gradually over an extended period of time. They will mature and mellow so slowly that they might not even notice that a significant change is occurring. It can take years, and then they wake up one morning and look into the mirror and see a person quite different than the one who had inhabited their bodies previously. But for me, everything, and I do mean everything, changed all at once. It was on the evening of Saint Patty's Day in 1980 Anno Domini.

My mother had come to Ketchikan to help Fanny and me with the delivery of our third child, who, we were expecting to arrive any day. I had awakened cheerfully and dressed in new white shirt and a green polyester sport coat. I tied around my collar a beautiful wool tie which sported the green and red tartan of our ancestral clan and which had been a gift from dear Mother. The tie was of particular importance because it denoted our ancient and unique relationship to the McDonald clan.

In school that infamous day, I delivered a brief dissertation on the importance of Saint Patrick, and I extolled the privilege of we few good men and women who were blessed with being from the sound and proud stock of Irish-American emigrants. Later that evening mother and I feasted on my favorite meal, traditional corned beef and cabbage.

Fanny had not been feeling well because of the effects of late term pregnancy and she complained that the smell of the cabbage was nauseating to her. She said that she had something important to discuss with me and that after the toddlers were bathed we would need to talk.

It was a Friday evening and I was in the mood for celebration so after dinner I invited Mom to go up to the tavern and to enjoy an Irish whiskey. I donned a silly green derby made of cheap felt and, arm in arm, mother and I hiked up the road to the bar.

Once inside we were delighted by the rambunctious crowd. Silver and green shamrock garlands and paper cut-outs of Leprechauns enlivened the celebration. We settled into a booth and were delivered two hardy mugs of green beer and two shots of good Irish whiskey. With the foot tapping rhythm of Riverdance blaring through the smoky pub, and amid the laughter and jubilation of those good patrons, I felt that all was right in the world and began an informal disquisition on the merits of the holiday.

"Isn't it wonderful, Mother Dearest, that we can sit here and celebrate our family heritage surrounded by good music and friends; that we can sup from the cup of our ancestors and be proud our Irish traditions? Let's drink to the Irish, let's drink to the Emerald Isle and the Great Luck which has been bestowed upon us by our hallowed and benevolent saint and protector, Patrick, the Patron Saint of all of Ireland!"

"To Saint Patrick!" she said in response and she took a small and grimacing sip from her little glass of Jameson's. "But Willie Honey, you're not Irish."

The whole bar seemed to instantly hush and I felt the stares of the patrons as they turned their heads in unison to eye us suspiciously. "What do you mean, Mother? I *am* Irish! I was named after me great grand-father, James McCracken, from Dublin. You told me that yourself when I was but a wee lad." My voice cracked and my Irish brogue sounded weak and contrived.

"My grand-father, James McCracken, was a Scot" She replied. "He made his way to Dublin, Ire-

land where he boarded a steamer and arrived at El-
lis Island before moving into Oklahoma Territory,
and then was a Sooner during the land grab. Didn't
you know that, Honey? His daughter, my mother,
married my father, Lorenzo McDaniels, who was
also a Scot, but was given the name Lorenzo in
honor of a traveling Presbyterian minister named
Lorenzo whom my Grandmother McDaniels ad-
mired. I'm sorry that you misunderstood but, Wil-
liam, you're not Irish, and there you have it." She
said stubbornly.

"What about my luck? Mom, you don't even
know how many times I've relied on The Luck of
the Irish."

"Luck of the Irish!" she sounded incredulous.
"There is no such thing as the luck of the Irish!" she
spat. "The potato famine, civil war, British domi-
nance, and the Irish ghettos, there's your Luck of
the Irish. You should be happy to be a Scotsman!
Listen up, Buster; any blood that you got from me is
good, Scottish blood so learn to live with it. It's a
good thing, believe me, for I am older and wiser
than you.

"Of the first there can be no doubt, but as to
the wiser, that's debatable. Some mother you are,

and on Saint Patrick's Day no less." I was sulking now.

When we arrive home I just wanted to crawl into bed but Fanny needed to talk. "I think we should raise the kids as Catholics," she proclaimed. "I'm the one who takes them to church every Sunday. If you would take them to the Lutheran church, things might be different but you always want to go fishing or hunting on the weekends so I've been taking them to Holy Name each Sunday. It's a nice congregation, and the kids need to be baptized soon. Will, are you even listening to me? I've signed us up for baptism classes beginning this Sunday after mass."

Well, there you have it. The rest is history. Since then, little by little, I've learned to live with my new ancestry. I, myself converted to Catholicism about two decades ago. Now I have guilt. I have adopted St Andrew as my patron. Andrew is the patron saint of Scotland. I've developed a taste for single-malt scotch (which is like mothers' milk on my palate) and have pasted a decaled flag of Scotland on the bumper of my minivan. My tartan tie still works because, as it turns out, the McDonald clan was from the county Argyll, in the highlands near Edinburgh.

Our daughter, Briana, was born just a few days after that fateful night and when she grew up she joined a troop of Scottish dancers. My son plays the bagpipes. I attend Robert Burns Night annually, and eat heartily of the haggis. I've even read some of his poetry and have learned the words to Auld Lang Syne.

I've noticed some of the less-than-marvelous characteristics of my new lineage in the bushiness of the wiry hairs that have been sprouting from my ears and eyebrows. Scotsmen have very bushy eyebrows. I've also developed the thrift of a Scot and now I can't seem to part with a single nickel.

As for luck, I've still got it. But, because I don't trust it as much as when I was an Irishman, (We Scots have trust issues.) I have come to rely on it much less frequently now than I did when I was young.

And I'll always be proud that I *used to be Irish.*

"We twa hae paidl'd in the burn,
Frae morning sun till dine;
But seas between us braid hae roar'd,
Sin' auld lang syne."

When Tom the Cob Stayed Late

Mum stewed upon her mushrooms
Burnin' bolts at Tom the Cob,
Who's alight with all the boys at Milly's Bar.
"Oh where's the Cob?" she sometimes cried
As if her man had never lied.
While Tom was drinkin' Guinness from a jar.
Oh Lord!
That Cob was drinkin' Guinness from a jar.

Her peacock tears flowed down one night
Through sodden burlap tapestries of scorn.
While Tom, in merriment got tight
And vowed that he'd stay out all night,
Then with his jibes he bent the Deacon's horn.
My stars!
And with his jibes he bent the Deacon's horn.

Then Milly sang her Mountain songs
The words were right but the notes were wrong
And her vixen wiles encouraged men to leer.
She sang and danced   'til nearly dawn
Then with the goody patrons gone
She poured 'em all another round o' beer.
That Lass!
She poured   'em all another round of beer.

When Tom, 'e finally shoved his glass
And set his tilted cap for bed and home
Old Mum was settin' in a ditch
And strippin' willows for a switch
Then met him half way 'cross the village green.
Beneath the brutal stingin' lash
Tom felt that Mum had grown too rash
And pondered how she'd ever grown so mean.
That Cob!
He pondered how she'd ever grown so mean.

The Mass of Fog

"How little do they see what is,
who frame their hasty judgments upon that which
seems."
Robert Southey

A thick fog hung down upon the sunless coast. Vaporous mists collected the early morning sounds and expelled them muffled and softened into the cloudscape of southeast Alaska. This was a gray world, a monotonous haze of lethargic values. And silent; even as his breath was exhaled, it was absorbed into the foggy April dawn. He stumbled along the slate-strewn beach, slipping on the kelp, stopping on the barnacles, balancing himself between earth and sky; belonging to neither and lost in both. He carried the mast of his sailing dingy over his shoulder. Its small sail was wrapped around the boom and lashed to the mast at an untidy angle. In his other hand he balanced two wooden oars to steady himself against the lingering effects of the inebriating liquor and to help secure him on the slippery stones.

The tide had receded far out and he had followed. He felt chilled by the dampness of the morning and his thin white jacket did little to warm him. He slipped and fell, bruising his knee on the shale. He struggled back to his feet then slipped again on the wet seaweed. This time, when he fell he dropped the mast. The boom crashed into the rocks and sent him sprawling. He tried to catch himself but was too slow to react and smashed into the rocks, his shoulder hitting hard followed by the side of his head. Again the man fought back up to his feet and gathered his mast, the boom, and the oars.

In the fog, with the low water line barely visible, the traveler limped through the monochromatic landscape, an element of his own design, unframed in a blur of impressionistic chaos.

He set the mast and boom on the rocks near the water's edge then laid the oars across them. He faced the water and fished a crumpled pack of Camels from his breast pocket. He ripped at the foil, letting it flutter to the shiny black rocks at his feet. He was tired and stiff but he knelt down to pick through the scraps of paper because among them had fallen a matchbook cover with a hand-scrawled phone number. Maggie had given it to him earlier when they had lain in her bed talking; when she had told him that she was checking in to a rehabilitation center. She needed to regain control of her life, she said, she needed to get clean. The phone number was to a clinic in Seattle.

He knew he was going to miss her; miss their wild Saturday nights, her laughter and her pretty face. "I'll call you on my way home to Oregon," he'd promised. But now, as he read the number on the matchbook, he doubted if he would ever call, or if he would ever see her again. An unemployed artist and a strung out junky made for a fragile couple. Three weekends together was the longest time either one of them had devoted to another person for a very long while.

Mary sat impatiently at her apartment window waiting and hoping that he would appear on the beach. She'd caught just the briefest glimpse of him two weeks earlier. His long hair and unshaven face had seemed somehow comforting and familiar. The following Sunday she'd seen him again. That morning, too, had been a foggy one. Her curiosity piqued as she had watched him stop to pray as he pushed a little boat down the rocky beach before disappearing into a fog.

Now, on the third Sunday, he arrived again. He appeared at dawn just as she was preparing to leave for the early mass at Holy Name Church. From her third story window, Mary watched him struggle down the beach shouldering his heavy cross. She cried out as he slipped on the kelp and fell hard on the rocky beach. She felt tears well up in her eyes as he knelt reverently. She saw the smoky incense of fog mingling around him until he was almost completely hidden by it. Dressed in white, he seemed to glow in the translucent fog. "And his clothes became as white as the light," Mary recited from the Book of Mathew 17:2. She could hardly make out what he was doing but because she had often prayed The Stations of the Cross she could easily envision this Passion Play; a beaten man, forced to carry his own cross. But even in her imagination she had never witnessed a more moving scene.

Out on this rocky beach, along this rain swept coast, here was a holy man. This was the man she would follow. Here was someone she could love. She felt it as deeply and with as much conviction as she held for the many aspects of her faith; the virgin birth, the resurrection, the sanctity of the church. Mary was faithful to her beliefs. She was a servant of God and would respond to His calling.

He lit his cigarette. Smoke slipped out from his nostrils and blended into the atmosphere. His head throbbed from the liquor, and the smoke, and from and the night of transgressions with his woman, Maggie. The silence of the fog intensified the pounding in his heart and in his head. He felt his blood ebb and flow through his neck and chest like the beating of a drum.

A pair of harlequin ducks eyed him curiously. He enjoyed observing the great variety of shorebirds feeding along this rugged coastline. He had sketched them often and so it had become his habit to carry along some bread or crackers to feed to them. He reached into his dirty coat pocket and pulled out the crusty dinner roll that he'd saved from the soup kitchen. He bit off a chunk to calm his stomach and tossed the rest to the birds. He felt inside his other breast pocket and pulled out the half-pint flask of cheap whiskey. He raised it into the air, toasting the ducks with a mock salute before putting the bottle to his lips. He took a long slug then spun the cap back on. The smoky liquid seemed to warm him for just a moment. To his soul, he thought, if he had one.

Mary watched with wondrous astonishment as the man communed with nature. Was he a priest that he could perform the Holy Communion? "And when supper had ended he took the wine and he drank from it giving you thanks and praise." She made the sign of the cross then knelt down on the hard linoleum floor of her apartment. She rested her interlaced fingers on the window ledge, "Take this, all of you, and drink from it," she recited, "This is my blood, the blood of the new and everlasting covenant, shed for you and for all so that sins may be forgiven. Do this in memory of me."

Suddenly, with his head thrust back and his arms out as if to embrace the world, the man cried out to the fog. It was a wild bellowing yell, coughed up from his atheist soul, blown through smoke tarnished lungs to a God that he didn't believe in. It was an acknowledgement of himself, from and by himself. It was a 'Good-bye' to Maggie, a 'So long' to Ketchikan and to Alaska. "I'm finished!" he cried. But the sound died as it left him, unsettling the ducks and agitating a curious raven, who called in response, "Kluklook." Then the raven glided down to the shoreline and into the fog, disappearing like the scream, like a dream, across the water and into the mist, black into white.

The man climbed up the shoreline and found his skiff where he had left it the night before; drawn up on the rocky point, hidden in the spruce and devils' club above the high tide flotsam. He gathered some thick branches from the ground and used them to skid the boat down the beach and into the water.

Mary heard him cry out to God. "It is finished." She recited John 19:30. "When He had received the drink, Jesus said, "It is finished." With that he bowed his head and gave up his spirit."

Hearing the man cry out the words of her dying savior stirred within Mary a great sense of urgency. She was suddenly impassioned and could wait no longer. She had to know who the man was. Mary clamored down the three flights of stairs. Nearly falling, she slid around the banister in the foyer. When the heel separated from her shoe, she stumbled forward, and although she'd painfully twisted her ankle, she was able to catch herself and kept from falling by skipping athletically through the lobby. She kicked off both of her shoes as she flew passed her neighbor, Mr. Thomas, who quietly raised an eyelid to the overzealous woman.

Bare footed, she hobbled outside and ran across Tongass Avenue, protecting her bare arms and shoulders with her hands and crossed arms. The thin blue dress gave little protection from the cold fog. She hurried along the side of the road searching for an access to the beach. But she was too late.

He set the mast in its step and let the boom fall down into the boat. There was not a breath of wind so he left the sail furled in the bilge like a shrouded corpse. He kicked off from shore and settled himself down on the transom bench. He leaned over the water, looking down into its steely depths. A starfish, purple and white, disappeared beneath the shadow of the skiff. A dungeness crab startled by the quiet boat, scuttled away and vanished into deeper water. "This water", he thought, "is the life force. This water is the only tangible god." He scooped some into his cupped hand, and looked into it, "This is the birthplace of life." He held the seawater close to his face and smelled it. It had the smell of life in it. "Tears," he said and then he raised his hand and he let the water fall through his fingers and run onto his cheeks. He realized that he was still drunk from the night before.

With his right hand he smashed a mosquito on his forehead, then wiped his hand on his stomach, and checked his breast pockets for his flask and cigarettes. He placed the oar-pins in their sockets, rowed out to the sea, and slipped into the fog. Turning back toward the sleeping town he raised his hand as a farewell to Maggie. As he looked back he caught a brief glimpse of someone in blue up near the roadbed. Suddenly, he was enveloped by the thick fog. Had he seen someone climbing down the rocks near the road? He shook his head to clear out the hangover but the vision was lost. "Maybe the cops want me for something," he thought, "better just keep rowing."

The fog opened up to him and closed behind him. He rowed the short stretch across the Tongass Narrows on water as smooth as glass. He rowed after the raven, rowed to his squatter's cabin on Pennock Island, rowed to find his few belongings and to catch the southbound ferry.

She watched him settle into his boat and she observed him as he baptized himself.

"Is he a priest," she wondered, "to be able to baptize? If he is a priest, I will join him, but I suspect that he is something much, much more," Mary whispered into the fog. She emulated his movements as he made the sign of the cross and then the holy man turned and looked toward her. He raised his hand and pointed to Heaven before vanishing completely into the whiteness. "I must find this man," she thought. "I feel myself loving him with all of my heart."

She climbed up from the beach and limped back toward town feeling renewed and invigorated. God had chosen her to be His witness. Her long hours of prayer and devotion had garnered for her witness to a great presence. She felt the comfort of her beliefs envelop her like a warm quilt.

Mary walked home to put on some shoes then went to mass. She confessed her sins and took Communion. A song played over and over in her head, "Here I am Lord, Is it I Lord? I have heard you calling in the night. If you lead me I will go, Lord. I will hold your people in my heart." She prayed for the holy man of the water, and she prayed *to* him.

"Next Sunday," she vowed, "I'll be waiting on the beach before dawn and, God willing, I will meet this man and I will devote myself to serving Him."

The Mobius Spirit

Drink the water from the river,
Soul filled soup of the spirit,
Of the forgiver.
From tributaries, and estuaries,
And the sanctuaries of God.

Sip the precious particles,
Delicious molecules,
Bound and unbound
Since creation,
Distilled by the winds,
Renewed in heaven.
Ingested, digested, expelled,
Evaporated, collected,

Brought to your parched lips,
The draft of saints,
Or a mammoth's drink,
From the cells of the beast,
Or Nefertiti's spa,
Taste the ionic solvent.
Refresh yourself.

Cleanse your soul in the baptizing bath.
From the holy waters
Of The Jordan, or The Thames,
Or the lowly creeks and nameless glades.
Relax in the slippery warmth
Of these very atoms;
Once the drops in Jacob's well,
Or a mothers anxious tears.
The broken water.

And blood and water issued forth,
Birth, and life, and joy.
Juice of our existence
Trickling through time.
And shocked to life
By only God

Breathe now the air transformed
By a thousand-thousand respirations.
Inhaled and exhaled
For countless millennia,
From lung to leaf,
Gill to goldenchain.

The hot breath of a scolding argument,
Or a lover's anxious pant.
A euphony of resonance
Warm and moist against
The goose-bumped flesh.

A whispered rosary
Created from light
In flora and fauna,
Bestowed to animals
To breathe, sing, hoot,
Howl, chirp, and pray it.
And return it to the green,

One to another and back again,
A symbiotic grace.
Breathed since a time
The sea was shocked to life.

And the ages piled up
Like the stones of Jehoshaphat.

Beat your chest and slap your cuffs
Free from the crematory dust.
Enshrouded by the dander
Of galactic mass,

Each miniscule speck
Alight with creation.

Where once stars were born
There formed ours and us,
Of the self-same stuff as suns.
The elements of them
Are the elements of us.

They exploded
and scattered themselves
Becoming the bread
And the live meat
Of this wet rock,

To spread their seeds,
To create, and re-create, and recreate.
To give Love and to receive it.

We cling to life
Like thistles to wool.

Feel the pulse of life.
The energy not lost nor gained
But changing form.
Rearranging forms of God to Man,

And God to Woman,
and back to God.

Ashes to dust, to stars.
Stars to light, to dust, to us.

Mountains crumble to stones,
To sands, to sediments.
Are folded, and baked,
And thrust up again
Into mountains.

The tide comes in and goes out.
The moon is new, then waxes,
Is full, then wanes.
Is new again.

And I find you here.
Created in this nebula
Of space and time,
Composed of the stars,
Drinking the waters
That Moses drank,
Breathing the transformed air,
And shocked to life
By only God.

The Living Water

With each easy breath a sense of peace spread through his body. He grew more restful, more profoundly quiet. He was alive and was enjoying the feeling. The sunlight warmed the side of his face and a gentle breeze caressed his cheek. His eyes were closed and swimming in a sea of vibrant crimson and orange. He felt the pulsing beat of his heart in his chest, and on his neck against the starched collar of his white shirt. He knew the miniscule airborn movements of hairs on the back of his hand, and the breeze which swayed the wispy, grey hairs across his forehead. He touched the worn leather binding of his *Constant Companion*. The book lay cradled in his hands. The fraying silk ribbon that held his place and divided its pages, softly tickled, web-like, on his pale wrist.

He inhaled the fragrances of spring. The new crocus sprouts and budding daffodils stretching up from the dark, rich soil. He heard the twitter of little birds and the mechanical drone of honey bees searching for pollen. But then he felt something else, a new presence, as if something or someone had joined him on the solitary bench in the quiet cemetery.

Squinting into the sunshine his eyes adjusted to the brightness. He gasped audibly as he beheld the figure of a man sitting close by, and who seemed to be studying him with unabashed intensity.

"Do not be afraid," said the visitor. His voice was soothing and foreign.

"Forgive me," he started. "I mean, excuse me. I …I didn't hear you arrive."

"And yet you knew that I was here. Didn't you? It's wonderful, these perceptions you have. How can a man feel it when he's being watched? I have often been amazed by these unnamed senses. Why haven't they been analyzed scientifically? It's a power we haven't even begun to understand."

This was an unorthodox way to present oneself, thought the man. At once he was suspicious of the new comer, but at the same time was curiously compelled to engage him in a conversation. And he found himself intrigued by the handsomeness and mannerisms of the silver-haired gentleman.

He seemed oddly out of place. Though dressed with obvious distinction and impeccably groomed, the eccentricities of his introduction, or lack thereof, caused the man with the book to be on his guard.

None the less, he reasoned, if introductions are to be made, he would take the leading roll. And so to direct the conversation toward a more con-servative and appropriate beginning, he stood and extended this hand. "Permit me please, my name is Malcolm, Malcolm Whitman."

The stranger stood in response and taking Malcolm's outstretched hand in a cordial grip, he looked deeply into his eyes and said, "The pleasure is all mine Malcolm, I assure you. I've been watch-ing your case with great interest for these past months. I'm very pleased with the prognosis for your complete recovery. I've traveled from Rome with the express intention to interview you about your ordeal and especially to ascertain your knowledge of the properties of water."

Malcolm was shocked by this turn of events. The familiarity, the strange questions and even more, this strange person's failure to introduce himself, lacked any semblance of civility and had become irritating. His voice cracked with annoyance, "My knowledge of the properties of water? Who are you, sir, and how are you acquainted with my case?"

"I am given to understand, through correspondence with your parish priest, Father Gorgeous, that you have recently made a miraculous recovery from a lethal form of lung cancer. You were diagnosed with stage IV lung and bronchial cancer that had metastasized to you liver. The prognosis was severe was it not?"

"My priest?" Malcolm was incredulous now. "What is this? Tell me who you are this instant and hope that I don't call the authorities. You have no right!" He tore his hand from the strangers grasp.

The stranger became immediately apologetic. "Please forgive me Mr. Whitman, my manners are inexcusable, a symptom of prolonged isolation and solitude. My name is Father Michael. I'm here on a research sabbatical from the Vatican."

"Are you a doctor, Father Michael? Why would Father Gorgeous discuss my illness with you and disregard the implied confidentiality of our private discussions? This is all very upsetting."

"Again, I apologize and I assure you that my interest in your case will remain confidential. I am not a medical doctor but hold advanced degrees in Bio-Chemistry and Molecular Biology, as well as Theology. My life's work, my Magnus opus, if you will, is to prove the physical presence of miracles and, more importantly, to determine how miracles are performed. My years of study, sequestered in the vaults and libraries beneath the Vatican, have caused my manners to atrophy into the atrocious condition in which you find me now. But I assure you, my inquiry is genuine and my hypothesis earth shattering. Please, sit down and speak with me, Malcolm." And then the holy man, with a sweep of his arm, directed Malcolm to be seated. To which the stupefied gentleman immediately complied.

Malcolm Whitman had been raised as a devout Catholic. He had attended Catholic schools and graduated from Gonzaga University. He was a fourth degree officer in the Knights of Columbus, a fraternal organization dedication to the protection of priests and widows. His wife, Martha, of thirty-two years was buried here, in this Catholic cemetery alongside his parents and his only son Jared, who had been killed by an IED while stationed in

Iraq. Malcolm loved his church. She was like a mother to him, reliable, unchanging, and always accepting. For his devotion he was also obedient and faithful. When he learned that this man, Father Michael, was on a mission from the Vatican, he immediately put aside his uneasiness and felt compelled to be helpful in whatever way he could. He sat back down on his bench, as if in a pew, ready to hear a homily from this most unusual priest.

"I see that you read the Bible," said Fr. Michael gesturing to the book in Malcolm's hands. "Wonderful, then you must have noticed the numerous references to the importance of water as it relates to the many miracles described by the sacred text. Have you made the connection between water and miraculous intervention? Jesus' first miracle was to turn water into wine at the wedding in Canaan, was it not? John baptized with water as do Christian priests throughout the world to this very day. The Sacred Eucharist is a blend of water and wine. Jesus even described himself once as *The Living Water* in the parable of the Samaritan woman at the well. And at his crucifixion he is lanced by a soldier and blood and water issued forth!"

The strange priest had become more and more animated as he presented example after example.

"The list goes on and on," he exclaimed, "and from the very beginning! God breathes His Holy Spirit into the waters in Genesis. And in Exodus the waters of the Nile run red with blood. Then there is Moses parting the Red Sea and drawing water from a stone in the desert."

The priest was now ranting uncontrollably. His face had reddened considerably and his voice had become high pitched. He waved his arms in such an aggravated display that Malcolm backed away and assumed a defensive posture. He thought that this man, who had so dramatically transformed himself from a slightly eccentric old priest to a raving lunatic, had absolutely and certainly gone insane. It was time to make an exit.

Malcolm stood and tried to steady his voice, "Well, this is all very interesting Father, but I'm afraid that I'm late for a very important appointment and I really must be going. Good day to you, Sir," and he spun about on his heel and began to depart with the longest strides he could muster without actually breaking into a lope.

"You were drowned as a child… Pronounced dead in fact!"

Malcolm stopped.

"Don't you understand, Malcolm, all of the ancient holy men had the power to manipulate the properties of water. Water is the essence of the Spirit."

"What does any of this have to do with me?" Malcolm felt himself growing angry. "Your crazy infatuation with water… I was a child. I didn't drown. You're over-reacting."

"Father Connelly was there. You were in pool filled with school boys. No one noticed that you were gone until they called all of the boys out of the water and discovered you lying unconscious at the bottom of the pool. And then as they all watched, the water began to move, *like a whirlpool*, as Father described it. You were lifted to the surface and washed up onto the cement beside the pool. Connelly was astonished. He classified it as a miracle. You were pronounced dead by the paramedics." Father Michael said while flipping through his small notebook.

"Of course they continued to try and resuscitate you all the way to St. Vincent's. The doctors there did everything in their power, but finally gave up and you were wheeled down to the morgue. Father Connelly was waiting there to meet your mother when you walked out, naked but for the tag on your toe. You were in a kind of trance and when your mother came in she ran to you and picked you up. That's when you seemed to awaken...when her tears splashed onto your cheeks."

"Ridiculous!" exclaimed Malcolm. Cold water drowning victims often recover even after prolonged unconsciousness. That is a medical fact and not a miracle."

"And the wave?"

"I don't know. Maybe I simply floated to the surface. Father Connelly was probably hysterical at the possibility of having just lost one of his charges. People don't think straight under those kinds of traumas."

"At any rate it was reported to my predecessors as a miracle. The church takes such reports seriously, as you can imagine. The report was filed, an interview was conducted, and then the matter was forgotten... until this new development, your miraculous recovery from cancer."

"These things happen all the time. You of all people should know that. No prognosis is a death sentence these days."

"Yours was. As of today you are the one and only survivor of this type of cancer, discovered at such a late stage. And the doctors have no explanation. Your recovery seems absolute, the cancer is simply gone. Do you believe that God saved you from the cancer?"

It was a question Malcolm longed to know the answer to. His had been a *miraculous* recovery. The word was used to describe his remission by every oncologist he had met with. Miraculous... the implications were humbling. "Why me?" thought Malcolm. "What have I done to deserve this?"

"Yes", he answered honestly. "And like many other victims of a life threatening disease, I prayed for strength."

"Forgive me for asking but, to whom did you pray?"

"God of course, and to my savior Jesus Christ, to the Holy Spirit, and sometimes to Mary, that She might intercede on my behalf."

"I see. This all comes down to the topic of my research," explained Father Michael, "The manipulation of molecules on the atomic level, specifically water molecules."

"Water," the priest continued, "the most abundant molecule on the Earth's surface. It is referred to as the universal solvent. Given the right circumstances, it can dissolve almost any polar molecule and most organic substances excluding oils and waxes. It is an ion, meaning that it has an electronic charge and a magnetic polarity. By changing water, breaking its hydrogen bond for example, it will seem to disappear, but in reality becomes a mixture of two explosive gases."

Malcolm was in no mood for a chemistry lesson. This day had started so pleasantly and now it had become a disaster. He decided that he must put an end to this nonsense.

"I don't wish to seem rude. I really don't, but I have no interest what-so-ever in your chemical bonds or your theories..."

"If a man, or a god, could control water, control it with his mind, let's say through telekinesis, then that man could perform miracles. To move water would create a flood or part a sea. He could impart taste or color by increasing its absorbency. By breaking the hydrogen bonds, water is removed, causing droughts, turning flesh and bone to dust, or to pillars of salt. Add a static discharge and you've created a burning bush or a deluge of fire from the sky. Thunder and lightning are both influenced mostly by the moisture in the air. Why do angels appear in clouds? Why, when Christ died on the cross, did the sky turn dark with storm clouds? Every miracle in the Bible can be explained by a force capable of changing or manipulating H2O on a molecular level. And I believe that you, Malcolm Whitman, are in possession of such a power!"

"I couldn't save my wife," cried Malcolm, "or my son."

"Your wife's illness was related to obesity, Malcolm. Fats are non-polar molecules that don't respond to water. During baptism sacred oils are applied to the child's forehead. Their resistance to water has always intrigued holy men and women."

"And my son was killed in Iraq. I didn't even know about it until several days later..." Malcolm's voice began to quiver. "When I became ill I would visualize a power surging throughout my body. The power would locate the tumors and pull them apart. I could see them being dissolved. I meditated like this for several weeks and began to feel better. When I stopped going to my appointments for chemo the doctors just thought that I was too far gone for the treatments to be much help. Father Gorgeous was my only confidant..." Malcolm's eyes began to well up. He clinched his Bible tightly and asked, "But, what of God?" He collapsed back onto the bench and hung his head behind a raised arm.

"We are of the same elements of God," answered Father Michael soothingly. "We are of the water. It sustains us and we are born of it from our conception in the womb. It is our primordial soup; it is the one constant element for the beginning of all life. You can control some small measure of it Malcolm, but you are not God... God is water but He is also light."

For the first time in his life, Malcolm began to cry. He loosed the water from his eyes. He felt the first tear form and roll down to the end of his nose. He watched it as it fell through space and spattered in the dust between his feet. Another tear formed and fell, and then another, and another.

A tiny rivulet of tears began to form. It ran downhill through the dusty earth and disappeared into the green grass of the cemetery.

Father Michael recited a verse from Song of Songs 8:7,

"Many waters cannot quench Love."
Rivers cannot wash it away."

Applauding the Bow

The curtains parted
Shredding sheets of silver rain
Played by the wind.
While the stallions shook the froth
Before their manes.

Tempting sisters
Danced in unison.
(The choreography in jazz)
And spun a sheen of raven hair
To block the sun.

A whirling trance of frenzied dancers
Leapt and ran before the wind.
As curling waves of gradient-green
Held fast.

In the wings
The Lancers lifted pikes
Parading off to war.
While ancient drummers
Pounded to the score.

Then fade to grey.
The tone diminished
With the aria complete.
And the hero
Finally sheathed his angry sword.

While the distant clapping thundered,
Golden-rayed and shimmer-wet,
 Our Lady made her entrance
With the sun.

She softly touched the mortal man
To calm his twisted brow.
Then she beckoned all the actors
To applaud the vessel's bow.

Ovation!
 To applaud the stalwart bow!

Fallen

From living in the pines she stopped beside a mountain stream, dense with graying alder on its banks. She paused to note the veining twigs of lace sewn through the sky, for gone was every summer leaf but one. And as she watched, the autumn breeze caught and shook that last leaf free. She strained to hold it in her sight, the whirling, swirling leaf in flight. Her eyes would not abandon as the golden leaf fell through the naked boughs. She marked the place it softly lit, and hastened there to gather it, the last of light and summer fallen down. Then knelt to pick her treasure up, but all were still and none stood out. So it was lost among the many fallen leaves. And that was all it ever took to loose her melancholy strings, a single, precious, fallen leaf not found. I held her close the night she fell, but lost her in her muted cell among the many other fallen lives. And that was all it ever took, a single, precious, fallen life not found.

Ravenous

Gently curved to hallowed space,
Beneath the collarbone,
Below the waist.

No apparition she,
Nor dream of feathered fingers
Belly stroke and preen

Denying touch without
But not within the cloistered orbs,
And muted sighs
Of unrepentant men.

Blue of White

Drawn the dusky,
Grey-faced sky.
Fenced in lattice,
Thin and rigid skins
That crack and peel.
Too late to seed
Before the skeletons
Break free and bury
In the snow.

To toss,
From opaque night
A stranger light,
Translucent.
Grieving for the loss
Of warmth.
They venture, squinting out
Among the shackled pain.
Avoiding others
Softly.

Depressions,
Briefly coated,

Crunch like bones
Beneath the boot.
While gelded mounds,
And swollen drifts
Engorge beneath the white
Pastoral gown.

Exhale

Today the weeds were singing.
Wasn't it of Truth?

But long before the great whale
Of the telling was still unborn.
In the silent rawness
Of no harsh call to seek and mate,
While the cry was held inside.

Confined for lack of rhythm and rhyme,
When bird songs lilted hollow.
Still trapped in quivering throats
Intent for a pause in the quiet.

A moment before the trilobites raged,
And pondered, but kept to themselves.
And the steaming bacteria,
Absolutely sincere,
Composing their wordless opinions,
Dissolved in the primitive soup.

When darkness pervaded,
Brooding to mature.
And the particles scattered.

Depolarizing the attraction
That started it all.

When all was arranged
And the universe still,
Wasn't it there?
Alone in the silence
Inhaling…
To bring the first sound
That started it all?

Causing everything to change!

…So long ago,
Before the screaming buffalo.

She Only Left..

She only left
Some empty
spice tins
stacked
… redandwhite
   redandwhite

Boxes of forgotten dreams
Collecting only dust.

The frigid winter
Cedars stand
hard-rooted
…holdingfast   …holdingfast
To memories.
Clutching to past promises.
(I clutch this ridiculous glove.)

She also left
A single glove
Single love
Singleglove
Uselessuseless singlelove

She's surely out there
All alone.
Her left hand growing
Coldandnumb and coldandblue
Andcoldandblueandnumb.

The low November sun
Aligns stark winter shadows
Rowuponrow
Shadows of widows
Rowuponrowuponrow.

Imprisoning this frozen
Land she left.
Swallow the sorrows of arrows.
Thearrowsinswallowsandsparrows.
That pierce this frozen heart
She left

Sorrowsofarrowsinswallowsandsparrows.
….She left.

..She left.

Listen Here

Listen Here.
The land, and sea, and sky
Are intermingled here.
Are symbiotic here.

The Spirit world,
So thinly veiled,
Transfigured here.
Finely crafted totems
Stacked, one upon another.
Until, from age to age,
The Tale is told,
When ancient turns
To present here.

Listen to the Stories,
Whispered and sung
To the rhythm
Of the universe.
By Heron
On the rocks,
She knows them each
By heart.

Raven beats
His hollow drum
To echo through
The mists of Time.

And great Whales sing
In unison.
While all the island's
Shallow-rooted Trees
Dance and stomp and
Listen Here.

Down the Windswept Cliff

Down the windswept cliff she flies,
A cape of grey through angry skies.
As freedom warms her terror-shock,
Her lips assume a smile to mock
The God before her eyes.

What sorrows shamed her none shall know.
Her heart was in a tantrum though.
While those who knew her strove to show
That given time she might outgrow
Her melancholy sighs.

What governs actions so distraught?
Surrendered life and love for naught,
And leaving but a stain of grief
On those who still contest the thief
Whom God and man despise.

So I, who loved her, must forgive
And find a gentler way to live.
To somehow readjust my course
But yield to sorrowful remorse
Awakened by her cries.

I drink this saddened cup in sips,
If I could once more kiss her lips…
The edges of my heart frayed rough
That given love was not enough
And so within me dies.

October Winds

Withered fruits decaying fall
Relieving equinoxal vines
Hue the contrast
Sucked from tangles
Scrambling tone to scale
And fight for graying light.

Broken shards of glass reflecting
Line the faces in the creases
Whiskered fields
Across the prickling grass
Arrange symmetric
Leafless age and stone.

Crisping lips of petals fallen
Scattered paper-weed from gutters
Cinders burn for drying eyelids
To the windy sweeping brushes
Pass to autumn.

Pressing time before the clock
Within the doubting faithless skins
The loosened threads unravel

Fearful faces tremble tilting
Freezing rain and pelting
Darkness on the wind.

That Place

I long to see
That place again
Someday.
It shall have
A gentle yellow glow,
A deep blue sky,
Alive with dancing trees.
It will be warm,
When finally I return.
My aching knee
Won't slow me then.
My vision will be clear.
Yes, I'd like to see
That place again
Someday.
And when I do,
I hope to see
You there.